STEPHEN DANDO-COLLINS

CAESAR

the war dog

operation
pink elephant

RANDOM HOUSE AUSTRALIA

A Random House book
Published by Random House Australia Pty Ltd
Level 3, 100 Pacific Highway, North Sydney NSW 2060
www.randomhouse.com.au

First published by Random House Australia in 2014

Addresses for companies within the Random House Group can be found at
www.randomhouse.com.au/offices

National Library of Australia
Cataloguing-in-Publication Entry

Author: Dando-Collins, Stephen, 1950–
Title: Caesar the war dog: operation pink elephant/Stephen Dando-Collins
ISBN: 978 0 85798 168 4 (pbk)
Series: Caesar the war dog; 3
Target audience: For primary school age.
Subjects: Dogs – Juvenile fiction.
          Detector dogs – Juvenile fiction.
          Elephants – Juvenile fiction.
          Poachers – Juvenile fiction.
Dewey number: A823.3

Cover photographs: dog © Ruth O'Leary/ruthlessphotos.com; Hercules C-130
© Dennis Steen/Shutterstock.com; savannah landscape © ligio/Shutterstock.com;
African elephant front-on © Talvi/Shutterstock.com; African elephant in profile
© Vaclav Volrab/Shutterstock.com; dry season © iStock.com/dave_valler
Cover design by Astred Hicks, designcherry
Typeset by Midland Typesetters, Australia
Printed in Australia by Griffin Press, an accredited ISO AS/NZS 14001:2004
Environmental Management System printer

Random House Australia uses papers that are natural, renewable and recyclable
products and made from wood grown in sustainable forests. The logging and
manufacturing processes are expected to conform to the environmental
regulations of the country of origin.

For Louise, who has trained me well.
With grateful thanks to Richard and Zoe.
And for the many fans of Caesar the War Dog *who*
couldn't wait for the next adventure to begin: Seek on!

CHAPTER 1

As the Australian Army Bushmaster bumped over the desert terrain, the soldiers in its crowded passenger compartment were smiling. All except for one.

'You guys want me to believe that Australia has more camels than any other country in the world?' said the odd man out, frowning in disbelief. Wearing camouflage pants and tunic, and a flat, peaked US Marine Corps cap, he was Major General Alan 'Bud' Weisner, and he had joined an Australian Special Forces patrol to watch the Aussies at work. He looked around at the seven other men – all of whom wore helmets, sunglasses, leather gloves and desert-patterned combat gear.

'It's a fact, General,' said a short, lithe SAS trooper sitting directly opposite, a man known to one and all as Bendigo Baz. 'Even more wild camels than in an Arab country.'

'Afghans migrating to Australia in the nineteenth century brought them to carry their loads across the desert,' said Corporal Lucky Mertz, the fair-haired

1

soldier sitting next to Baz. 'They let them run wild. The boy camels and girl camels just kept having babies, so the population grew and grew.'

General Weisner shook his head. 'Next, you'll have me believe that this here dawg can talk.' He nodded to the alert brown labrador sitting between the legs of Sergeant Ben Fulton. The dog had been watching each speaker in turn.

'In a way, sir,' said Ben, the dog's handler, 'Caesar can talk.'

'You just have to be tuned into his wavelength,' said Sergeant Charlie Grover, the troop leader, who sat by the Bushmaster's rear door. 'Ben can read Caesar like a book. And I can sometimes get the gist of what he's trying to tell us, too.'

'Caesar was Sergeant Grover's care dog for a while, sir,' Ben explained.

'Until I mastered my Zoomers,' said Charlie.

'Mastered your what?' said the general.

'My Zoomers, sir,' Charlie returned. He bent down and rolled up one trouser leg to reveal a carbon-fibre prosthetic leg.

General Weisner gaped at the sleek black Zoomer. 'You're on active service with a prosthetic leg?'

'No, sir, not *a* prosthetic leg,' Charlie replied, before rolling up the other trouser leg to reveal a second Zoomer. '*Two* prosthetic legs.'

Several of the Australian soldiers in the Bushmaster laughed at the general's astonishment. They were used to Charlie's Zoomers and, like Charlie, never gave them a second thought.

The general shook his head. 'You Aussies! A Special Forces sergeant on prosthetics, more camels than anywhere else in the world, and a talking dawg!'

The Bushmaster suddenly slew to a halt.

'Contact!' yelled the vehicle's commander. 'Hostile with RPG at eleven o'clock!' Swinging the roof-mounted machinegun to the left, he opened fire.

Charlie's smile quickly disappeared. 'Dismount left and engage!' he called above the machinegun chatter, unbuckling his seat harness. He opened the Bushmaster's rear door and sprang out into the sunshine, carbine at the ready.

The six other Australian soldiers were close on his heels. Caesar came bounding out with Ben, who kept him close on a short leash. General Weisner was second-last out the door, with Baz last of all, pushing the general in the back with one hand, to hurry him up, and lugging his favoured Minimi machinegun with the other.

Outside, the men quickly fanned out to the left of the stationary Bushmaster, whose gun had fallen silent. They threw themselves flat against the side of a dune three metres high, flopping onto red-tinged sand that was baking-hot. Caesar dropped down beside Ben, tongue hanging out in the searing heat, and tail wagging – this, to him, was fun. A second Bushmaster that had been following forty metres behind them also came to a halt, and another eight Special Forces troops spilled out the rear and took up positions against the dune.

'The Bushmaster's .50 cal has dealt with the RPG,' announced Charlie. 'Ben and Caesar, scout ahead for IEDs. We'll cover you.'

'Roger,' Ben returned. He lowered his head to his labrador companion. 'Ready to go to work, mate?' he asked Caesar.

In response, Caesar licked Ben on the cheek and gave him a look that seemed to say, *Ready when you are, boss.*

Ben smiled and gave his canine mate a solid pat. 'Okay, Caesar. Seek on!' Up he rose, and Caesar did the same.

With Caesar on the leash, padding over the sand just ahead of Ben, the pair moved past the first Bushmaster as it sat immobile, engine ticking over. Behind handler and dog, Charlie and the others were slowly sweeping the landscape with their weapons, ready to open fire to protect Ben and Caesar from attack. Heat shimmered off the sand. Keeping the dune on their left, dog and handler cautiously moved forward. Ben held the end of Caesar's leash in his right hand, and cradled a Steyr automatic rifle with the other.

General Weisner lay unarmed in the middle of the group of Australians, watching dog and handler with interest. Only now did the general notice that Caesar had leather booties tied to each of his paws. 'You gotta be kidding me!' he exclaimed. 'That dawg is wearing booties!'

'Special footwear for explosive detection dogs, General,' explained Charlie. 'A place as hot as this, with baking sand underfoot – that's not a dog's natural terrain. It's not ours, either, but at least we've got thick boots to protect our feet. So, the Special Operations Engineer Regiment came up with something to protect the EDDs' feet in places like this.'

'Now I've seen everything. Dawg booties!' said Weisner, with a laugh in his voice. He watched Ben and Caesar working their way forward. 'They been together long, that dawg and his handler?'

Without taking his eyes off the landscape, Charlie nodded. 'Ben picked him out at the kennels when Caesar was about eighteen months old. They've become like father and son.'

'Personally,' said General Weisner, 'I don't think a combat unit is any place for a dawg.'

'That dog has saved our lives more than once, General,' said Baz, sighting down his Minimi.

'Yeah, but just the same –' Weisner responded.

'Caesar's onto something!' called Lucky. He had been watching Caesar and Ben's progress through the telescopic sight atop his Blaser sniper rifle.

Sure enough, a hundred metres ahead of the first Bushmaster, Caesar had come to a halt. With his head low, he gazed at the side of a tall ridge of sand. All of a sudden he dived forward and began to dig furiously with his front paws, sending sand spewing out behind him. His tail was wagging furiously.

'No, Caesar!' Ben growled, hauling back on the leash.

Caesar stopped digging and turned his head to Ben. The puzzled look on his face seeming to say, *But I found something!*

'You know what to do, Caesar,' scolded Ben.

Caesar ducked his head and let out a little whimper, as if to say, *Oops! Sorry, boss.* Then he promptly sat and gazed intently at the spot where he'd begun to dig. Sand rolled down from above to partially fill the hole he'd created. This stare was Caesar's 'signature', the way he signalled the location of hidden explosives to Ben.

'That's better, mate,' said Ben, ruffling the labrador's neck. He then dropped to his knees and, shouldering his rifle, slid a gloved hand into the sand where Caesar had been digging, then rummaged about until he felt an object about ten centimetres in. Pushing the sand aside with both hands, he revealed a package the size and shape of a shoebox. In fact, it was a shoebox, painted a sandy colour to blend with its surroundings. Carefully, he removed it from its hiding place and sat it on the sand. Giving Caesar a pat, he said, 'Good job, mate. You found it.'

Caesar, happy that he was back in Ben's good books, began to wag his tail anew.

Coming to his feet, Ben looked back to his waiting comrades and signalled for them to approach. Three of the SAS men came at the trot, before Charlie, Lucky, Baz and the general followed. Meanwhile, the men at the second Bushmaster remained in covering positions.

'What's your dawg found there, Sergeant?' the general asked as he joined the group standing around the EDD and his handler.

By way of explanation, Ben dropped to one knee and took the lid off the box.

Major General Weisner peered into it and scowled. 'What's that in there?' he asked. 'Looks like a sugar sachet to me.'

The box was empty but for a white square sachet.

'It is a sachet, sir,' said Ben. He held it up to show the general. 'An EDD training sachet. It contains chemicals typically used in explosives.'

'And that's what your dawg sniffed out, through the sand?' Major General Weisner reached for the sachet.

'I wouldn't touch it with your bare hands, if I were you, sir,' said Ben, holding onto the sachet.

'Why's that, Sergeant?' the general demanded.

'You might set off an explosives detector when you go through airport security on your way back to base tomorrow,' said Ben, half jokingly.

'Or Caesar might track you down as an insurgent,' Baz suggested with a smirk.

Weisner looked around at Baz. 'I touch that, and the dawg could track me down?'

'Yep,' Baz said with supreme confidence.

'As much as twenty-four hours later,' added Ben.

Weisner turned back to him. 'That, I would like to see, Sergeant. And your dawg was able to detect this, through the sand! Outstanding, soldier. Outstanding!' He glanced at Caesar, who was staring intently at the sachet. 'He's trained to dig up his finds as well, huh?'

'Er . . .' Ben looked embarrassed. 'Actually, General, that's a bad habit of Caesar's. He's not supposed to dig, though he loves nothing better than to dig up my mother's rosebushes. He's trained to indicate the location of explosives, but once in a while his enthusiasm gets the better of him and he will dig for them. This is our first op since we got back from overseas, so he's keen to please.'

'Yeah, Caesar's only human,' said Baz, getting a laugh from the others.

'Caesar's digging habit was what attracted you to him, wasn't it, Ben?' said Charlie.

'That's right.' Ben dropped the sachet back into the shoebox and closed the lid. 'The digging habit showed he had an intense curiosity, and that's what we need in a good EDD.' He gave Caesar a pat and stood up.

Charlie, meanwhile, checked his watch. 'Okay, let's

call it a day. Back to the LZ.' Turning to the two Bushmasters and the men with them, Charlie twirled a finger in the air, then pointed back the way they had come. 'Exercise terminated.'

This had been a training exercise, part of the induction of several new men into the SAS Regiment. The sighting of an RPG by the Bushmaster's commander had been fictitious, but apart from that, Charlie had striven to keep things as real as possible every step of the way. The day before, an army helicopter had landed here, and one of the crew members had buried the shoebox containing the explosives sachet. The helicopter pilot had noted the location via GPS, and the commander of the leading Bushmaster had been given the coordinates to follow.

Caesar and the sixteen Special Forces men piled back into the Bushmasters. They were soon headed south toward an area on the flat twenty kilometres away, which was being used as a helicopter landing zone.

'So, this is Australia's Simpson Desert,' said Major General Weisner. 'I've never seen so much sand in all my days.'

'Largest sand dune desert in the world, sir,' Baz volunteered.

'176,500 square kilometres, to be precise,' added Lucky. 'It straddles the corners of South Australia, Queensland and the Northern Territory.'

'You guys are full of facts,' said Weisner, a hint of derision in his voice.

'We study hard before every mission, General,' Lucky said seriously. 'We have a cardinal rule in the SAS – learn as much as you can about the place your unit is tasked to operate in, before you set foot there. That information might just save your life one day, or the life of someone you've been sent to rescue.'

The major general nodded. 'I know the value of good intel, Corporal,' he said to Lucky. 'But where do you draw the line? When do you say "Enough, too much information"?'

'You can never have too much information, sir,' said Charlie.

'For instance,' said Baz, 'did you know that the Simpson Desert is named after a fridge?'

For a moment there was a stunned silence in the back of the bucking Bushmaster.

'What he means, sir,' said Lucky, 'is that this desert is named after Alfred Simpson, who founded a washing machine company that became the largest whitegoods company in Australia.'

'Simpson!' said an SAS man, his face lighting up. 'My mum and dad have got a Simpson fridge at home.'

'Same bloke, same company,' said Lucky.

'The ironic thing is,' said Charlie, 'Lucky's expert knowledge is not going to benefit the SAS much longer.

His enlistment is up in a week, and he's leaving the army.'

'Is that right?' the major general said with surprise. 'That's a shame. Got another job to go to, Corporal?'

'Yes, sir,' Lucky replied. 'I'm joining the Tanzanian Wildlife Service, in Africa.'

'Hell's bells!' Weisner exclaimed. 'That'll make for a heck of a big change. From Special Forces to playing nursemaid to wild animals.'

'Not really, sir,' said Lucky. 'I grew up among animals. My father is a zoologist in New Zealand. But it's my military skills the park rangers want. There's a war going on over there, between ivory poachers and the rangers – and the poachers are winning. They're better armed and better led than the rangers. My job is to turn that situation around.'

'Well, good luck, Corporal,' said Weisner sincerely. 'What about you other guys – you're going to miss the corporal, right?'

'Nah!' said Baz, with a wink Charlie's way. 'Lucky's the last bloke you want to go on ops with – he farts in his sleep.'

This brought a roar of laughter from the others.

'We will miss Lucky,' said Charlie. 'He's been my right-hand man for quite a few years now. But I know he's passionate about animal conservation. I think he'll do a great job in Africa.'

'I'm passionate about chocolate,' said Baz, grinning broadly, 'but I wouldn't want to work in a chocolate factory.'

This brought more laughter from the men. As the banter continued, Ben leaned down to Caesar and spoke quietly in his ear. 'You did good today, mate. But we have to get you out of the digging habit. If that had been a real IED there in the sand, you might have set it off.'

Caesar, looking around at him, let out a whine as if to say, *Sorry, Ben*, then licked his master on the end of his nose.

Laughing, Ben pulled Caesar's head in close for a cuddle. 'I can never be mad at you for long, mate.'

Lucky reached over and patted Caesar. 'In my book, this four-legged bloke can do no wrong. He's the best!'

CHAPTER 2

'Where's Caesar?' Ben asked, taking a bottle of water from the fridge.

'Out in the backyard, playing with Maddie,' said Nan Fulton, while peeling potatoes at the kitchen sink.

'Just keep an eye on him,' said Ben. 'He's started digging again. He did it on an exercise in the Simpson Desert last month, and he did it yesterday while we were training new EDDs at Holsworthy.'

'He'd better not start digging up my rosebushes again!' Nan peered out the kitchen window, then began to laugh. 'Ben, come and look at this!'

Ben took a swig of water and joined his mother at the window. A broad smile creased his face. 'Will you look at that!'

Maddie, Ben's daughter, was playing with Caesar on the back lawn. The chocolate labrador sat there patiently, wearing a hat and sunglasses, as Maddie put one of her summer dresses on him.

'So cute!' said Nan, touched by the sight. 'Caesar will let Maddie do anything with him.'

'I wonder what the other war dogs would think if they saw Caesar in a dress,' Ben said with a chuckle.

'Dad! Nan!' came Josh's voice from behind them.

The two of them swung around to see Ben's son standing in the kitchen doorway, holding his laptop.

'What is it, Josh?' Ben asked.

'I found a clip of Lucky talking about his new job. You've got to see it! We've all got to see it!' Josh hurried to the door and yelled, 'Maddie, come see Lucky in a video.'

Maddie looked up and frowned. 'Lucky? Lucky who?' she called.

'Our Lucky. Come on, it's important!'

'Oh, *our* Lucky? In a video?'

Lucky Mertz and Bendigo Baz were close friends of both Charlie and Ben. All four of them had served together in Afghanistan. They had fought alongside each other in the very battle during which Ben and Caesar had become separated. Caesar had been lost for more than a year. Lucky and Baz had sometimes come with Charlie to visit the Fultons, and Lucky always brought sweets for Josh and Maddie.

'Come on, Maddie!' Josh urged. 'Lucky's saving the elephants!'

'Elephants!' Maddie jumped up and ran to the house.

Josh set his laptop on the dining table, and the rest

of the family gathered around to watch. On the screen, three men stood in front of a large map of Tanzania and surrounding African nations. One of them was a bulky, bespectacled African man dressed in a smart business suit and tie. The other two wore green military-style uniforms.

'There's our Lucky!' Maddie cried with glee, pointing to him. She crawled up onto a dining chair to be closer to the screen, just as the African man in the picture began to speak.

'My name is Benjamin Kadanka, and I am Tanzania's Minister for Natural Resources and Tourism,' he said. The minister was perspiring freely and was clearly nervous about speaking to camera. He cleared his throat. 'Under the control of my ministry are the fourteen national parks, thirty-eight game reserves and forty-three game-controlled areas of my country. Between them, they make up twenty-eight per cent of the territory of Tanzania.' He turned to the two men beside him. 'With me today I have Tanzania's Chief Ranger, Mr Wallace Springer, and his new Deputy Chief Ranger, Mr Lucky Mertz. Chief Ranger Springer, who is also President of the International Ranger Federation, will now address you.'

Springer, a solid man of medium height and sporting a neat beard, took a step closer to the camera. 'The killing of elephants for their ivory tusks has been illegal in Tanzania since 1989,' he began in a broad Australian accent. 'Yet, poachers have killed forty thousand elephants in this country every year for the past three years. Forty per cent of the country's elephant population has been slaughtered during that period. At this rate, within ten years there will be no more elephants left in Tanzania. Not one!'

'Not one?' said Josh.

'That's hobble!' exclaimed Maddie. 'Why would anyone want to kill elephants?'

As if to answer Maddie's question, Chief Ranger Springer continued. 'The elephants are being killed for their ivory. The poachers kill the elephants, cut off their tusks and leave the carcasses to rot.' As he spoke, footage of slain elephants filled the screen.

'Hobble, hobble, hobble!' Maddie cried.

'It's okay, princess,' said Ben, putting his arm around her.

'No, it's not, Daddy!' Maddie retorted, snuffling back tears.

'The ivory is smuggled out of the country in containers and shipped to East Asia,' said Chief Ranger Springer. 'There, the tusks are used in the extensive ivory-carving trade, and are ground down for traditional Chinese medicines. Ivory smuggling is now as profitable as the trafficking of illicit drugs. It's worth billions of dollars.'

'Wow!' said Josh, looking at his father. 'That's incredible, Dad!'

'It's hobble, that's what it is!' Maddie reiterated.

Minister Kadanka spoke again. 'Over the past decade, more than three thousand park rangers have been killed by poachers.'

'These poachers,' Chief Ranger Springer resumed, 'are very well organised, armed and trained. They act like an army. In fact, the largest group of poachers calls itself the Revolutionary Army of Tanzania, or RAT. They claim to be freedom fighters who only poach ivory to fund their revolutionary operations.'

'But they are nothing more than bandits!' Minister Kadanka interjected.

'The Tanzanian Government has now authorised me to fight fire with fire,' said Springer. 'Deputy Chief Ranger Mertz, until recently, was a highly experienced soldier with Australia's famous Special Air Service Regiment. He has been tasked to train our rangers in Special Forces techniques and lead the fight against the poachers. Lucky, would you say a few words?'

Lucky stepped forward. 'Thanks, Wally. In the past, the poachers have had the upper hand against the rangers,' he said to the camera. 'Many rangers didn't even have proper boots. They frequently had no radio communications and were armed with antiquated weapons. Now, we're equipping mobile anti-poaching squads with the best gear, the latest weapons and fast overland transport. And this is my message to the poachers: If you keep on poaching, my men and I will track you down. You will be caught, and you will spend the rest of your days in jail. You have been warned!'

'Yeah!' Josh cheered.

'Well done, Lucky,' said Nan, with pride in her voice. 'That's a really important job he's taken on.'

Maddie turned to her father. 'Will our Lucky get the hobble poachers and save the elephants, Daddy?'

'If anyone can do it, Lucky can,' Ben assured her.

'Lucky is about the coolest Special Forces guy there is,' agreed Josh. 'Apart from you, Dad – and Charlie.'

'If Lucky doesn't do it, Daddy,' said Maddie, 'you have to promise that you and Caesar will save the elephants. It's dericulous what the poachers are doing. Someone has to stop them!'

Ben smiled. 'That's what Lucky is over there to do, sweetheart,' he said. 'He's got it all under control. I don't think Caesar and I would be able to make much difference.'

'Talking about Caesar,' said Nan, 'what's he up to, I wonder?' She headed back to the kitchen. Moments later, she let out a shriek. 'Oh, no! He's doing it again!'

'Doing what?' Ben asked, hurrying to the kitchen, with Josh and Maddie on his heels.

'Digging up my roses!' Nan wailed.

Peering out the window over the kitchen sink, Ben began to laugh.

'What's so funny, Daddy?' Maddie asked.

Ben picked her up so that she too could see out the window. 'Look,' he said, grinning and pointing to the garden.

There was Caesar, busily pawing away the earth around the base of a rosebush, still in bonnet, sunglasses and dress.

'It's not a laughing matter, Ben,' Nan protested. 'Stop him!'

'Okay.' Ben set Maddie back down. 'But first,' he said, reaching for his phone, 'I have to get a picture of Caesar decked out like that! No one would believe me if I told them.'

It was several weeks later. The sun was setting, sending purple and pink streaks across the western sky. In the distance, an Australian Army Tiger attack helicopter hovered fifty metres above the ground, the cannon beneath its nose pointing toward a rundown brick barn that was missing half its roof.

From the west, three Black Hawk helicopters whisked in at treetop level, one behind the other, mere black blobs against the sun. They stopped so abruptly their noses lifted up briefly, making them look like bucking broncos. There they hovered, level and stationary, above the dry, flat earth. Rappelling ropes tumbled down from either side of each Black Hawk, and heavily armed SAS men came sliding down in quick succession. Each man was clad in black, a gasmask covering his face.

Once their passengers were all on the ground, first one, then two Black Hawks lifted, banked and flitted away, heading back the way they had come. Meanwhile, the third chopper remained. Ben Fulton slid down a rope from one side of it, and Caesar was rapidly lowered from the other. Both wore gasmasks – with Caesar's being specially made for war dogs. As soon as the pair were on terra firma, the last Black Hawk wheeled away.

'Inform HQ that insertion is complete and we're going in,' Charlie instructed the group's signaller, a man with a heavy VHF radio pack on his back and a large aerial jutting into the air above it.

'Roger that!' the radioman returned.

The SAS men ran toward the trees at the crouch, quickly spreading out as they advanced. Ben and Caesar loped along behind. At the same time the Tiger helicopter moved forward, and as it passed over the top of the barn, several canisters dropped from beneath it. Moments later, grey clouds of tear gas swelled up through the roof opening.

The men had surrounded the barn in seconds. Some had dropped flat and lay with their weapons trained on the barn's door and windows. Like Charlie, several were positioned on one knee.

'Time for Caesar to do his thing, Ben,' said Charlie.

'Roger.' Ben unclipped Caesar's metal leash and spoke quietly in the labrador's ear. 'All the way around the barn, mate. See what you can find.' Standing up, he commanded, 'Seek on, Caesar!'

Leaping forward, Caesar bounded toward the barn.

Charlie now spoke into the personal radio attached to

the top of his black Kevlar bulletproof vest. 'EDD going in. All eyes peeled!'

Ben eased down onto one knee and watched his dog's progress, occasionally letting out a piercing whistle. He had a different whistle for 'Go left', 'Go right', 'Forward', 'Back', 'Return' and 'Return quickly'. Caesar recognised every whistle and reacted immediately to each, almost as if Ben had him on an invisible string.

Caesar trotted along the front of the barn, his tail wagging slightly, before turning down the building's right side and disappearing around the back. Ben always felt uneasy when Caesar was gone from view. He preferred to have his four-legged mate in his line of sight. But the SAS men posted on the other side of the barn knew to report if Caesar found anything, in which case Ben would hurry to join his EDD.

Caesar reappeared along the barn's left side, trotting with his nose down. A battered old Land Rover was parked nearby, under the shade of a ghost gum tree. The Land Rover's front passenger door hung open. Caesar did a quick circuit of the vehicle, then sniffed its interior. When he dropped back onto all fours, Ben knew that Caesar was satisfied the Land Rover was 'clean'. He whistled for Caesar to return. Caesar took several paces toward Ben and stopped. His head came around, then he turned and headed for the ghost gum.

'Is he going for a pee?' asked Baz.

'I don't know what he's up to,' Ben confessed, intrigued, 'but Caesar always has a reason.'

Charlie nodded. 'Roger to that.'

When Caesar reached the tree he stood up on his hind legs, with his paws on the white trunk, and looked back at Ben. Then he dropped to the ground and sat there, staring intently up into the ghost gum.

'Caesar's found an IED in the tree,' Ben stated categorically. 'It's probably sited to detonate when anyone goes near the car.'

'*In* the tree? Someone has been very creative with their bomb planting,' Charlie remarked. He turned the switch on his personal radio. 'Be advised, there's an IED in the tree beside the Land Rover. Avoid both. Beta Team, enter the barn via the rear doors. Beta, go, go, go!'

Ben whistled the recall, and this time Caesar loped back to him immediately with his tail wagging furiously. 'Good boy, Caesar!' said Ben, ruffling the dog's neck. 'You found it, didn't you? Good job, mate!'

At the same time, there came the sound of automatic weapons fire from inside the barn. Only seconds passed before Beta Team emerged, dragging two men who had tears streaming down their faces. A third man, whose tied hands were being freed, was led out behind them – he had been held hostage by the others.

The radios on Charlie's and Ben's vests crackled to

life. 'Hostage secured,' said the leader of Beta Team. 'Two insurgents taken alive.'

'Roger to that,' Charlie said with satisfaction, coming to his feet and removing his gasmask. 'All units stand down. Exercise complete. Repeat, exercise complete.'

The SAS men holding the two insurgents let them go and, sharing a joke with them, proceeded to bathe their stinging eyes with damp cloths produced by the group's medic. The 'hostage' and the 'insurgents' were all SAS men, acting out the roles in a training exercise. On this occasion, they were in the bush north of Perth, Western Australia.

Training exercises are a part of SAS routine. Just as a football team will train for six days a week before its game day, daily life for Special Forces units not on frontline duty is all about training, training and more training. This is designed to keep their men sharp and in a constant state of readiness for the real thing, and to hone the skills of new members of the squadron.

The radio operator now came to Charlie and Ben. He pulled off his gasmask to reveal a puzzled look on his face. 'Just got a weird message for you guys and Baz.'

'What's the message?' Charlie asked.

'Rice for water,' the radioman replied. 'You're to report to RAAF Pearce right away. Any idea what "rice for water" means?'

Charlie looked at Ben. 'We sure do,' he responded with a wry smile.

'It's the GRRR activation code,' said Ben. 'Somewhere in the world, GRRR is needed.'

'Call in a heelo,' Charlie instructed the radio operator. 'Ben, Caesar, Baz and I need to get to RAAF Pearce. Fast!'

Ben, Caesar, Charlie and Baz strode across the tarmac from an army Black Hawk at the Royal Australian Air Force's Pearce Base in Bullsbrook, just outside Perth. The chopper had given them a ride in from the desert. In the background a pair of training aircraft from the Singaporean Air Force went streaking down the airstrip and took to the air. The Government of Singapore trained its pilots at Pearce Base.

When the quartet walked into the base's briefing room they were greeted by a man they knew well – SAS intelligence officer Major Alex Jinko.

'Good to see you blokes,' Jinko said warmly, after exchanging salutes with them all. 'And you, too, Caesar.' He gave Caesar a vigorous pat, and Caesar responded with a wagging tail.

'What's up, sir?' Charlie asked. 'We got the call from GRRR.'

'I'll let Captain Lee brief you,' Jinko said, turning and walking toward a large LED screen on the far wall. On the screen was an office with framed military pictures on its walls. That office could have been anywhere, but it was in fact halfway across the world in Manhattan, at the headquarters of the United Nations beside New York's East River. 'Captain Lee, are you there? Charlie Grover's team is here.'

A slender woman with very short hair walked into view and settled on the edge of a desk, facing the camera. In addition to being in charge of protecting the Secretary-General of the United Nations, Captain Liberty Lee was also Commander of the Global Rapid Reaction Responders, a small, elite UN unit founded by the Secretary-General. It was a unit to which Charlie, Baz, Ben and Caesar were attached, with the approval of the Australian Government. 'Hello there, gentlemen,' said Liberty.

'Evening, Captain Lee,' Charlie said with a smile, as he, Baz, Ben and Caesar joined Jinko in front of the screen.

'Thank you all for responding so quickly.'

'What mission have you got for GRRR, Captain?' Ben asked.

'Yeah, where are we headed?' added Baz.

'The mission is in East Africa,' Liberty replied. 'The secretary-general received calls from both the Prime Minister of Australia and the President of Tanzania, asking for the United Nations to help sort out a particularly tricky hostage situation.'

'It's a hostage rescue?' Charlie asked.

'That is correct, Sergeant Grover,' said Liberty. 'A rebel group calling itself the Revolutionary Army of Tanzania, or RAT, has taken a senior wildlife ranger hostage.'

'Where does the UN come in, Captain?' Ben asked. 'Can't the Tanzanian Army take care of the situation?'

Liberty sighed. 'I wish it were as easy as that, Sergeant Fulton. For one thing, while these RAT rebels operate for the most part in northern Tanzania, they move freely back and forth across the borders of neighbouring nations such Kenya, Rwanda, Burundi and the Republic of the Congo. International law prevents the Tanzanian Army from crossing those borders in pursuit of RAT rebels, so those rebels can always escape to other countries. And the governments of those surrounding countries are either unwilling or unable to capture them – they have their own criminals to worry about. This is a cross-border issue, an international issue. A UN issue.'

'And therefore a GRRR issue, ma'am,' said Ben.

'Precisely. There is also another international aspect to the problem. The ranger taken hostage by RAT is not Tanzanian. He has Australian citizenship.'

'An Australian citizen?' said Ben. He recalled the video that Josh had shown him only weeks before. 'Not Chief Ranger Springer?'

'No, not Chief Ranger Springer,' Liberty replied. 'I'm sad to say we all know the ranger involved very well.

He is a former member of the SAS and of GRRR. Your good friend Lucky Mertz.'

For a moment there was a stunned silence. Baz was the first to react. 'Not our Lucky?'

'I'm afraid so.'

'How could a highly experienced SAS man like Lucky be taken hostage?' Charlie demanded, incredulous.

'Apparently, RAT first captured several of Lucky's rangers. The rebel group threatened to kill the rangers unless Lucky surrendered himself to them.'

'Lucky voluntarily went with these RAT rebels in order to save his men's lives,' said Charlie, nodding to himself.

'It's the sort of thing he'd do, that's for sure,' said Baz.

'Where's Lucky now, Captain?' Ben asked.

'We have no idea,' Liberty admitted. 'The Australian and US governments are using all their technical know-how to try to locate the RAT and Lucky, but the hostages could be in any one of half-a-dozen countries by the time you get over there.'

'So, you're sending us over to rescue Lucky?' said Charlie.

'That is correct. Including yourselves, a GRRR team of a dozen men has been summoned. As there is a low likelihood of IEDs in the territory where you'll be operating, I felt it would only be necessary to have one EDD on this mission. Otherwise, it will be a standard GRRR deployment. The remaining members of your team are on their way to Western Australia from all parts of the world. You will all have your final briefing at Pearce Base in twenty-four hours' time.'

'How do we get to Tanzania, ma'am?' Ben asked. He looked at Caesar, who sat attentively with his head to one side while listening to the familiar voice of Liberty Lee. Ben was hoping the transport method would be the least stressful for his canine partner.

'That will be explained to you at the full briefing tomorrow,' said Liberty. 'I will tell you more then. Good night.' The satellite transmission ended, sending the LED screen to black.

Ben, Charlie and Baz looked at each other. 'Who'd have thought we'd have to save Lucky?' said Baz, voicing their thoughts.

'He spent his career saving other people's lives,' said Ben.

'What a reversal of roles,' Major Jinko remarked.

'Roger to that, sir,' Charlie agreed.

While Ben waited for the rest of the GRRR team to arrive, he took the opportunity to Skype his family. Caesar sat beside him with a curious look on his face.

'Here we are,' came Nan's voice, as her, Josh and Maddie's faces filled the screen. The three of them were sitting side by side on the sofa of 3 Kokoda Crescent, Holsworthy.

'Hi, Dad,' said Josh.

'Hello, Daddy. Hello, Caesar,' said Maddie. 'Where are you?'

Caesar put his paws on Ben's lap and looked at the screen, his head cocked to one side. His tail wagged furiously with delight at hearing the voices of the Fulton family. The tilt of his head told of his confusion at not being able to pick up their scents.

'Hi, guys,' Ben responded. 'Caesar is so excited to see you.'

'I can see him! I can see him!' said Maddie. She jumped up and put her face right up to the camera. 'Hello, Caesar! It's me, Maddie! Give Maddie a kiss, Caesar.'

Caesar, like most labradors and unlike breeds such as German shepherds, rarely barked. Instead, he let out a little whimper of frustration at not being able to smell Maddie. He licked the computer screen.

Ben chuckled and gently pulled Caesar down to sit beside him. 'Caesar kissed you on the screen, Maddie,' he advised, bringing a gleeful giggle from his daughter.

'Sit back down, Maddie,' said Nan, reeling her in with a tug of her skirt.

'What's happening, Dad?' Josh asked.

'Caesar and I will be heading off on an overseas op tomorrow, son,' said Ben. 'I thought we'd catch up with you now, before we go.'

'How long will you be away?' Josh sounded a little unhappy that his father would soon be out of the country again. He was accustomed to his dad going off on top-secret missions, sometimes for months at a time, but that didn't mean he didn't miss Ben.

'Yes, how long, Daddy?' echoed Maddie.

'Not long. A week, maybe.'

Josh immediately perked up. 'A week? Is that all?'

'A week's not long,' said Maddie, sounding equally pleased. 'Where are you and Caesar going this time?'

'You know I'm not allowed to tell you that, princess.'

'Yeah, it's all top secret, Maddie,' said Josh, chiding his little sister. 'Like always.'

'Oh, come on, Ben,' said Nan. 'Maddie and Josh have kept bigger secrets than this before.'

Ben sighed. 'I know, I know.'

'At least give us a clue?' Maddie implored.

'You don't have to tell us *exactly* where,' Nan added. 'We've known when you've been in Afghanistan and places like that.'

'Okay, okay,' Ben replied. 'All I can say is that Caesar and I will probably be seeing some really big animals with large floppy ears.'

'Elephants!' Josh exclaimed. 'You're going to Africa!'

'I never told you a thing,' Ben said with a smile.

Maddie gasped. 'Elephants! Africa? You and Caesar could save all the elephants from being poached!'

'Ah.' Ben realised he had said too much. 'I can't really –'

'Daddy, you've got to promise to save all the elephants, and come home in a week.'

Ben smiled broadly. 'Caesar and I will see what we can do.'

Twenty-four hours after the Australian contingent arrived at Pearce Base, the remaining members of the GRRR team assembled in the base's briefing room. For Caesar and Ben, this was a welcome reunion with men they'd operated with before, most memorably in Afghanistan when they'd rescued the UN Secretary-General from Taliban insurgents. That operation had been the catalyst for the creation of GRRR.

The first to approach the Australian EDD and his handler was Sergeant Angus Bruce, a Royal Marine Commando. 'There he is!' the Scotsman exclaimed with a broad grin on his face. 'The wee super-sniffing machine himself!' Dropping to one knee, he ruffled Caesar's neck and patted his flank, setting the labrador's tail wagging with delight.

'How are you doing, Angus?' Bensaid with a smile.

'Fit as the proverbial fiddle, Ben,' said Angus. 'But I'm sorry that it's rescuing Lucky Mertz that's brought us back together again.'

'No one would be sorrier than Lucky. He was always helping others. I think he'd be highly embarrassed by the predicament he's found himself in now.'

'Aye, but we have to treat this mission as if we didn't know Lucky. We can't let our personal feelings cloud our judgement about the job we have to do.'

'You're right about that, man!' exclaimed Corporal Chris Banner, a tall, powerfully built West Indian member of Britain's Special Boat Service, as he joined them. 'We have to be professional about this.' Grinning widely, he gave Ben's hand a firm shake. 'Good to see you, Ben.' He looked down at Caesar. 'And you too, Caesar.'

Men from other elite Special Forces units around the world were soon greeting Ben and Caesar. Ben shook hands with the three American members on the team – Sergeant Duke Hazard, Sergeant Tim McHenry and Corporal Brian Cisco. Then there was Sergeant Jean-Claude Lyon from the French Foreign Legion, German Army Special Forces medic Willy Wolf, and Toushi Harada, a computer expert with a top-secret unit of the Japanese Self-Defence Force.

As was the Japanese custom, Toushi was a very formal sort of person. Instead of shaking hands, he bowed to Ben and Caesar. He then produced a shiny packet from his pocket. 'I bring gift for my GRRR comrade Caesar,' he said, smiling. 'All the way from Tokyo.' Ripping the plastic wrapping, he took out a biscuit. The aroma from the packet immediately caught Caesar's attention, and when Toushi held up the biscuit, Caesar's eyes followed it as if he were hypnotised. 'Finest Japanese dog cracker,' Toushi said. 'Got fish and rice and all things nice. Okay for me to give to Caesar, Ben? All Japanese dogs *love* these crackers.'

Ben smiled. 'Sure, Toushi. If he'll take it.'

Toushi held the cracker out to Caesar. In response, Caesar looked at Ben for permission.

Ben nodded. 'It's okay, mate.'

Caesar sniffed the biscuit, then opened his mouth and politely took hold of it. In three crunches, it was gone.

'There, you see! He like very much,' Toushi said with pleasure. 'Here, you take, for Caesar.' He gave the remainder of the packet to Ben. 'I ask my family to send many more.'

Last of all to renew his acquaintance with Ben and Caesar was Corporal Casper Mortenson. From the Danish Army's Hunter Corps, Casper was an expert underwater diver. He shook his head as he took Ben's hand. 'Lucky Mertz was not so lucky after all, my friend,' he said, 'being captured by those African rebels.'

'Lucky was doing the right thing by his men, as he always has,' said Ben. 'Another man may not have given himself up to the RAT the way he did, to prevent his rangers from being killed.'

'I suppose,' Casper replied with a shrug.

'Atten-shun!' Major Jinko called from the front of the room. Every man came stiffly to attention as Major General Mike Jones strode to join Jinko.

'At ease, gentlemen,' said the general, commander of all Australian Special Forces units. 'Be seated, please.'

The twelve men of the GRRR team quickly found their seats. When Ben let go of his leash, Caesar knew that he was permitted to relax. He eased down in front of Ben, laying his chin on his extended legs. Every now and then Ben would see Caesar's ears rise or twitch as the labrador heard familiar names and terms. When Caesar's own name was mentioned, his head would come up or his eyebrows would ruffle.

General Jones now addressed the group. 'The Australian Government has acceded to a request from the UN to support a GRRR mission in East Africa,' he began. 'Before Major Jinko begins the briefing, there is someone in New York who wants a word with you all.'

Liberty Lee and the Secretary-General of the United Nations, Dr Park Chun Ho, appeared on the screen behind him. 'Hello, and thank you for coming, gentlemen,' Dr Park said with a smile. Tall, slim and dressed in a suit, he was an elegant-looking man with an air of serenity about him. 'You are about to embark on a very important mission – the rescue of your former colleague. Your primary concern must be the safe retrieval of Ranger Mertz and that of any other rangers being held against their will.'

Liberty Lee interjected at this point. 'We have reports that five other rangers – all local men – are being held with Lucky.'

'Let me say to you, gentlemen, off the record,' the secretary-general continued, 'if you are able to capture the leader of the Revolutionary Army of Tanzania – one Abraham Zuba, also known as Colonel Pink Eye – you will be doing the people of Africa a great service. Many of Zuba's so-called soldiers are mere children, some as young as ten years of age. He kidnaps them from their villages and presses them into service in his army, which he finances by selling elephant tusks to foreign ivory merchants. If you can apprehend Zuba while rescuing Ranger Mertz, RAT will disintegrate and those boy soldiers can return to their families. At the same time, a major threat to the elephant population of East Africa will be substantially reduced. Good luck with your mission. I know you will perform to your usual high standard. I shall return you to Captain Lee.'

Liberty Lee now took up the briefing. 'The UN has received approval from the governments of most of the countries bordering Tanzania for GRRR to operate on their soil, as long as we liaise with those governments. US spy satellites at this very moment have their lenses focused on the areas where we suspect Zuba and the

RAT are hiding out. By the time you get over there, we hope to have pinpointed where Lucky is being held. I'll update you with the latest intel once the mission is underway. Good luck, GRRR.'

'Yes, good luck,' the secretary-general echoed, before the screen went black.

'There you have your orders,' said General Jones. 'Extract Lucky Mertz, and if in the process of doing so you just happen to capture Abraham Zuba, that will be a bonus.'

'But be aware that, under international law, we have no authority to apprehend Zuba anywhere other than in Tanzania,' Major Jinko quickly added.

'A minor technicality, sir,' said Sergeant Hazard, bringing chuckles from the others.

'Any questions?' said the general.

'Sir,' Charlie called, 'do we have a codename for the mission?'

General Jones nodded. 'We do, Sergeant. Your mission will be known as Operation Pink Elephant.'

This brought smiles and nods from around the room.

'Pretty appropriate,' said Baz, 'considering this bloke Colonel Pink Eye is killing all those elephants over there.'

'Major Jinko will now brief you on what lies ahead,' said the general.

'Thank you, sir.' Jinko turned to the screen, which now came to life with an image of an African man wearing military fatigues and a red beret, cradling an AK-47 assault rifle. Thick wraparound sunglasses concealed his eyes. There was a faint smile on his lips. 'This is the only photograph we have of Abraham Zuba. Note his white hair. In Tanzania, the locals call him Colonel Pink Eye because Zuba has albinism.'

The men in the room looked at him blankly.

'You want to tell us what that is, Major?' said Hazard.

'Albinism is a congenital complaint that affects the pigmentation of one's skin and hair,' Jinko replied. 'It also affects the eyes of the individual.'

'Okay. You mean he's an albino?' said Hazard.

Jinko grimaced. 'Albino is not a term that the medical community likes to use these days.'

'You know what? That doesn't stop Zuba *being* an albino,' Hazard came back with a shrug. 'He's either an albino or he ain't.'

'Well, he does suffer from albinism,' the major continued. 'Sub-Saharan Africa has the highest incidence of albinism in the world, and it's very prevalent in Tanzania.'

'In practical terms, sir,' said Ben, 'what does that mean as far as Zuba is concerned? What should we be aware of?'

'As a man with albinism, Zuba is very sensitive to sunlight,' Jinko answered. 'He sunburns easily, and he has to wear dark glasses during the day. According to reports from Tanzania, he prefers to operate at night. And some say his poor eyesight renders him unable to read.'

'This revolutionary army of his, sir,' said Charlie. 'What are we up against? How many men does this Abraham Zuba command?'

'We know almost nothing about the Revolutionary Army of Tanzania. We know they are well armed with automatic weapons. They have access to four-wheel drive vehicles, so can move quickly from location to location. As for numbers, estimates of the size of his army range from fifty men to five hundred. When I say "men", two-thirds of them are boys.'

'Do they have a fixed base, sir?' Ben asked.

'Not that we're aware of,' Jinko replied. 'They seem to move around from one temporary camp to another, or they stay in villages and terrorise the locals.'

'How do they move the ivory out of the country, sir?' Angus Bruce enquired. 'Maybe we can track them down via the ivory merchants.'

Jinko smiled wryly. 'That's certainly an avenue we've begun to explore. We understand they send the ivory out of the country in shipping containers, buried in sacks of agricultural produce such as soya beans. But how they get the ivory from the plains to the ports is a mystery to us at this point.'

'The UN has asked Interpol to look into that,' General Jones interjected.

'And we hope to have all the intel sorted out for you by the time you land on African soil,' added Major Jinko.

'How do we get to Tanzania, sir?' Ben asked.

'That's an interesting problem,' Jinko replied. 'We need to insert you people by heelo, as close as possible to the rebel location. The Tanzanian Air Force Command doesn't possess large military heelos – just a couple of Bell Jet Rangers – and its heelo pilots don't have special ops training, so we can't use them.'

'Nor do we have the time to ship our own heavy-lift heelos over to Tanzania from here,' said General Jones. 'We could fly a couple of Black Hawks over in C-17s, but it would take up to a week to get them operational over there – and we don't have a week. The RAT is unpredictable. They could turn nasty on Lucky at any time.'

'We need our people on the ground over there pronto!' Hazard declared.

'Correct, Sergeant,' Major Jinko agreed. 'And when we looked at the alternatives, we had a bit of luck.' He pointed the remote control at the screen, and a picture of a massive grey warship appeared.

'Is that an aircraft carrier?' asked Jean-Claude, frowning at the image. The ship had a large flat deck and high sides.

'That, Corporal Lyon, is HMAS *Canberra*, the newest addition to the Royal Australian Navy's fleet,' said Jinko. 'She's an LHD – which stands for landing, helicopter, dock. Basically, she's a very large, very sophisticated helicopter carrier. At 27,500 tonnes, she's the largest ship ever to serve in Australia's navy. She's brand new, and right now, she's in the Indian Ocean on her working-up trials.'

'As we speak,' said General Jones, '*Canberra* is steaming at full speed for the coast of East Africa, to play a part in Operation Pink Elephant. Within twenty-four hours, she will be within heelo range of Tanzania.'

'*Canberra* is carrying heelos, sir?' Charlie asked.

Jinko nodded. 'On a full deployment, she can carry eighteen large heelos on her hangar deck, and another six or eight on the flight deck. Her working-up cruise will actually take her to Florida in the US by the end of the year, to collect two squadrons of brand-new Romeo heelos and bring them back to Australia. But she's already carrying a complement of Seahawks – similar to the Black Hawk and perfectly suitable for insertion missions. More importantly, their pilots have experience inserting Navy clearance diver teams on special ops, so you can be confident they know what they're doing when they insert you in the Tanzanian bushlands.'

'How do we get aboard *Canberra*, sir?' Charlie asked.

'Airdrop from a Herc,' Jinko replied. He broke into a grin. 'Assuming you can all parachute onto a flight deck two hundred metres by thirty-two metres.'

'Piece of cake!' exclaimed Sergeant Tim McHenry.

'Damn straight it is!' Sergeant Hazard concurred.

'With respect, Major,' Ben spoke up, 'I don't want to put Caesar in harm's way unnecessarily.' All the others in the room turned to look at him. 'If I were to make a hard landing on a pitching ship's deck, I'd come out of it okay. But Caesar might not. He isn't capable of breaking his fall the way I can. In an airdrop, he completely relies on me. And he could be seriously injured in a hard landing on a ship.'

'Can't have that, mate!' Charlie remarked with concern.

'Too right!' Baz agreed.

'So, what are you saying, Fulton? You'd rather we left Caesar and yourself out of the mission?' said General Jones.

'No, sir,' Ben returned. 'I'm saying that I'd rather jump into the sea with Caesar and make a soft landing. Can *Canberra* have a small boat standing by to pull us out of the water?'

The general nodded. 'Not a problem. If you want to take a dunking, that's fine by me.'

'Caesar loves going for a swim, sir,' said Baz, winking at Ben.

'We'll alert *Canberra* to have an inflatable standing by to pluck you and Caesar from the ocean, Fulton,' said the general. 'Any more questions from any of you?'

'What is our ETD, sir?' Hazard asked.

General Jones looked at his watch. 'Three hours

and seven minutes from now. A Herc from the RAAF's Number 37 Squadron will be landing here at Pearce any moment. Once it's refuelled and you people have kitted up, the Herc will fly you to the American base on the island of Diego Garcia for a refuelling stop. You will then fly on to rendezvous with *Canberra* at sea, somewhere north of Zanzibar, where you'll make your jump.'

'You'll receive your final briefing aboard *Canberra*,' Major Jinko advised. 'Meanwhile . . .' He held up a dozen waterproof maps, all folded to slip neatly into a pocket in their combat uniforms. 'Your operational maps of Tanzania. Study them. Baz, hand these around.'

Baz collected the maps from the major. 'Who will be giving us that final briefing aboard *Canberra*, sir?' he asked, as he distributed the maps.

'I will,' said Jinko. 'I'm jumping with you lot, and will coordinate your insertion and on-the-ground movements from the ship's operations centre.'

'Ha!' Tim McHenry said with a glint in his eye. 'Think you can land on *Canberra*'s deck, Major?'

'I may not have made a parachute jump in a while, Sergeant,' said Jinko, 'but I haven't forgotten how.'

'Okay, we'll see you on *Canberra*'s flight deck,' said McHenry. He nudged the man next to him, Brian Cisco, who grinned.

'Yes, you will,' said Jinko, definitely.

'As of this moment, gentlemen,' said General Jones,

'Operation Pink Elephant has "Go" status! The Prime Minister rang me personally to wish you good luck and good hunting. So, go get Lucky Mertz. And do me a favour – get Abraham Zuba.'

'Yes, sir!' all the men chorused.

In the darkness, Major Jinko, the dozen men of the GRRR team and an EDD tramped up the rear ramp of a bulky RAAF Hercules C-130J transport aircraft. Each man carried a heavy pack on his back, and most had a bag in one hand and a bulging parachute pack hanging from one shoulder. Ben Fulton had to handle all this equipment while also keeping hold of Caesar's leash. The packs and bags were filled with clothing and personal equipment that the men were likely to need on their African mission – light clothing for the tropical heat of the days, and warm black outfits for ops on cool African nights. Ground crew had already stowed metal cases aboard the Hercules that contained the weapons, ammunition and communications equipment for the group, all supplied by the Australian SAS. But every man had packed his own main and reserve parachute. Once packed, those chutes would never leave their sight until they jumped.

Apart from his personal equipment, Ben was toting

special gear and rations for his EDD partner. As for Caesar, he trotted up the metal ramp and into the bowels of the Hercules with his tail wagging happily. Caesar knew a Herc by both sight and smell. He liked Hercs. Almost every time that he and Ben flew on one, they ended up jumping out of it and parachuting to earth. Caesar adored parachute jumps!

'Here we go, mate,' said Ben, as they reached the webbing seats along the side of the fuselage where he and the other GRRR members would strap themselves in for the long flight ahead. 'Off on another mission together. Go say hello to the others,' he said, unclipping Caesar's leash.

Caesar padded around the interior of the Hercules, nuzzling in between Charlie and Baz as they talked, and receiving friendly pats from each. Other members of the team gave him a similarly warm reception as he moved among them, taking in their scents. Only Casper Mortenson, the Dane, showed no interest. Mortenson had once told Ben that he had never owned a pet of any kind and could not really understand why some people had more affection for animals than they did for fellow humans. Not that Mortenson mistreated animals. He simply didn't relate to them.

Caesar sensed Mortenson's disinterest and accepted it. He returned to Ben, his tail wagging contentedly. Ben knew that these few 'getting to know you' minutes at the start of a mission were important for Caesar. Taking in the distinctive scent of each member of the team, the labrador felt assured that he was among old friends and that he was accepted as a member of the team. To him, they were all now members of the same pack, like wolves setting off on a hunt.

The Herc's rear ramp was slowly raised. One by one, the aircraft's four Rolls-Royce engines whined to life and the six-bladed propellers began to spin. Ben, now seated in the webbing, reattached the leash to Caesar's collar. 'Okay, settle down, mate,' he said to his four-legged partner. 'We've got a long flight ahead of us. We should both get some sleep.'

Resting his jaw on his extended brown legs, Caesar lay at Ben's feet. When Baz sat next to Ben, Caesar hardly moved, merely raising his eyes to see who it was.

Baz, in good spirits as he buckled his safety harness in place, turned and punched Ben playfully on the arm. 'Lucky Mertz, here we come!' he declared. 'Watch out Colonel Pink Eye, GRRR's on its way!'

Diego Garcia was a small British-owned coral island in the Indian Ocean, 5000 kilometres northwest of Perth. Due west, another 3650 kilometres away, was the east coast of Africa and Tanzania, the destination of the GRRR team. The tropical island traced around a lagoon that looked like a giant footprint from the air. A number of US Navy supply ships lay at anchor in the shelter of the lagoon. On the eastern side sat a small military base and a desolate-looking airstrip operated by the US military, on lease from the UK Government.

Once the Hercules carrying the GRRR team had landed, the passengers crossed the concrete tarmac through blazing forty-degree heat, to air-conditioned buildings. There, in a US Air Force mess, breakfast had been prepared for them. Ben and Caesar were last in line as the hungry Special Forces men passed by a servery in single file with plates in hand.

An American cook in an apron and tall chef's hat looked at Ben and then at Caesar. 'What'll Fido have?' he asked with a wry smile. 'Eggs over easy? Fried tomatoes? Hash browns?'

Ben checked out the extensive all-day menu written on a blackboard beside the servery. 'How's the steak? Tender?'

'Most tender T-bone in all of Diego Garcia,' said the cook.

'Then both Caesar and I will have it.'

'Coming right up.' The chef chuckled to himself. 'Don't suppose the dog wants a knife and fork with that?'

'I'll be doing the carving.'

Sure enough, Ben chopped his EDD's steak into small, manageable pieces. Caesar lay under the table, downing his meal, as Ben sat eating and chatting with Charlie.

Before long, Major Jinko and the Herc's RAAF pilot Jennifer O'Shay joined them, carrying loaded plates.

'Squadron Leader O'Shay and I have just been talking on the radio to General Jones at SOCOM in Perth,' said Jinko.

'Weather conditions in the Indian Ocean are deteriorating,' the squadron leader informed them. 'It's looking like the sea state will be pretty bad by the time we reach *Canberra*.'

'How bad?' asked Charlie.

'Sea State 4 to Sea State 6,' O'Shay replied, before downing a mouthful of poached egg.

'What does that mean?' Ben asked.

'Sea State 6 means waves of four to six metres,' the squadron leader replied.

'How stable will *Canberra*'s flight deck be with swells of that size?' Charlie asked.

'There will be some deck movement, but not much,' said Jinko. He took a sip of his steaming-hot coffee. 'She's a big ship. We should be able to successfully parachute onto her. I'm most worried about Ben and Caesar. *Canberra* can launch her boats up to Sea State 4, and launch her heelos up to Sea State 5.' He looked directly at Ben. 'If worse comes to worst, a heelo could pluck you two out of the water. But if conditions do reach Sea State 6, *Canberra*'s heelos will be grounded. That means you and Caesar will be on your own in the water and in big trouble, with no boats or heelos to get you out. And in those sorts of seas, it will be almost impossible to see you two.'

'Trying to talk me out of jumping with Caesar, sir?' Ben retorted, pausing with a piece of steak on the end of his fork.

'I want to alert you to the risk involved,' the major answered. 'I won't be ordering you and Caesar to jump, Sergeant. It will be your call.'

'But there is a possibility it won't blow as hard as they're predicting?' Charlie interjected. 'You said Sea State 4 *to* Sea State 6, ma'am?'

'That's correct,' said O'Shay.

51

'How about we wait until we're over the DZ and see what the conditions are like?' Ben suggested. 'We can decide then.'

'Roger to that,' Charlie agreed. He didn't want to leave Ben and Caesar out of this operation if he could help it. He knew what a vital role both might end up playing in rescuing Lucky.

Major Jinko nodded slowly. 'Okay, we wait. But I don't want to have to explain to General Jones, or the Prime Minister, that we rescued Lucky at the cost of our best and most famous EDD and handler being lost in the Indian Ocean.'

'Don't worry, sir,' Ben said with a smile. 'I'll admit, before I became an EDD handler, there were times as a soldier that I threw caution to the wind. But now that I'm responsible for Caesar's life as well as my own, I will never put him in jeopardy. I'll always protect him, the same way he protects me.'

Jinko looked relieved. 'Good to know, Sergeant. Good to know.'

'We'll make three passes over the DZ,' advised O'Shay. 'Two at 1000 feet, the third at 2000 feet. Six men will jump on the first pass, six on the second. The EDD team will jump on the final pass, from 2000 feet – that will give *Canberra* plenty of time to eyeball you and get a visual fix on your point of splashdown.'

Ben nodded. 'Understood, ma'am.'

Jinko turned to Charlie, the mission leader. 'You're all good with that, Sergeant?'

'Copy that, sir,' Charlie acknowledged. 'All good.'

'As a matter of interest,' said Ben, 'what's the highest sea state rating?'

'Sea State 9,' O'Shay replied. 'That involves waves of fourteen metres and above. Officially, waves that high are described as "phenomenal".'

'I bet they are,' said Charlie.

'Cyclone conditions?' Ben mused.

'Exactly,' said the squadron leader. 'You don't want to be on the sea in any boat, no matter how large, in those conditions.'

'Fingers crossed for Sea State 4 by the time we reach *Canberra*,' said Charlie. He looked across at Ben, who nodded.

At Ben's feet, Caesar snorted, as if in agreement.

Five hours later on the bridge of the 27,500-tonne HMAS *Canberra*, the ship's commander, Captain Brian Rixon, focused on a single green blip on the aerial radar screen in front of him. The captain, a grey-haired man with thirty years in the navy under his belt, eased back in his chair. 'How close is the Herc now?'

'Blue Orchid now forty-one nautical miles due east of *Canberra* and closing, Captain,' a radar operator advised. Blue Orchid was the codename for the Hercules carrying the GRRR team. The aircraft was seventy-five kilometres away from the ship.

'Estimated ETA, Nav?'

'At our present speed and Blue Orchid's present speed, ETA seventeen minutes, sir,' the navigation officer replied.

'Very good.' Looking to the helmsman sitting beside him, the captain issued a command. 'Starboard twenty. Bring us into the wind.'

'Starboard twenty, sir,' the helmsman replied, gently turning a wheel that was much the same size as, and had a similar appearance to, a car's steering wheel.

As the ship slowly changed course, Rixon turned his attention to his air division commander, the fair-haired Lieutenant Commander Terry Lockhart, who stood by the vast bridge window. 'Prepare to launch ASR heelo, then clear the flight deck to receive visitors,' he ordered, coming to his feet.

'Aye, sir,' Lockhart responded. 'Prepare to launch ASR heelo,' he repeated into a microphone, relaying the message throughout the ship.

Captain Rixon walked to the bridge window on his left and looked down at the flight deck fifty metres below, where a blue-grey RAN Seahawk MH-60 helicopter sat with its rotors spinning. The ship shuddered faintly as it turned into the wind and ploughed into the rolling westerly swell. Rixon stroked his chin thoughtfully. 'What's the sea state now?'

'Right at the limit of Sea State 5, sir,' came the reply from the navigation officer behind him.

Rixon nodded and looked to the gloomy sky ahead. 'And likely to get worse,' he said, half to himself.

'We're at the limit of safe heelo operations, sir,' the air division commander advised.

'I'm aware of that, Mr Lockhart,' replied the captain. 'But the Met forecast is for increasingly deteriorating conditions in the next few hours. If we don't take delivery of the Herc's load now, they'll have to turn around and fly back to Diego Garcia. That will put Operation Pink Elephant at least twenty-four hours behind schedule, if not longer. What do you think, XO? Do we warn them off?'

The ship's executive officer and second-in-command, Commander Darren Shipley, came over to stand beside his captain. Five years younger than Rixon and balding, Shipley looked at the tip of the flight deck forward. Sea spray flew up from the bow and rained down on the deck. Again, the ship juddered faintly from end to end. 'The flight deck looks pretty stable to me, sir.'

'And to me,' Rixon agreed. 'Sea State 5 for air ops is a theoretical limit. This working-up cruise is supposed to test this ship's theoretical limits, and the flight deck is barely moving in these seas. Unless conditions worsen dramatically – and rapidly – we'll proceed as planned.' He turned to the air division commander and barked three instructions in rapid succession. 'Launch heelo. Clear the flight deck. And prepare to recover parachutists.'

'Aye, aye, sir.' Lieutenant Commander Lockhart spoke into his microphone. 'Launch heelo! Launch heelo! Launch heelo!'

Within moments, the Seahawk rose up from the deck and banked to the left. Flitting away from the big warship, it headed southwest before flying in an arc that quickly brought it astern of *Canberra*. Once there, it took up station following the LHD's white wake. A hundred metres above the swells, it crept forward, keeping pace with the ship as it pushed through the waves at its cruising speed of nineteen knots.

Meanwhile, the air division commander issued orders into his microphone. 'Clear the flight deck! Prepare to recover parachutists!'

'Message from Blue Orchid, sir,' reported a communications rating. 'Message reads: Are you ready to receive me?'

'Advise Blue Orchid that *Canberra* is ready and waiting,' the captain responded. 'Currently Sea State 5. And advise them of our new course.'

'Roger. Advising now, sir.'

In the spacious cockpit of Blue Orchid, pilot O'Shay was throttling back the four engines of the big plane, easing down from a cruising speed of 640 kilometres per hour to the much slower speed required for parachute drops.

In the rear of the Hercules, most members of the UN team were on their feet and helping each other strap on lifejackets, then parachutes, and finally equipment packs which sat on their chests or dangled from their belts. The only team member not receiving any special equipment was Caesar. Ben was carrying both their needs in his packs. And when they jumped, they would jump together, with Caesar strapped to Ben.

As the passengers prepared, the Herc's RAAF loadmaster pressed a button, and the plane's rear ramp lowered electronically. Slowly coming down to the horizontal, the ramp created a massive opening, revealing a grey sky and, flitting by 1500 feet below, an equally grey Indian Ocean topped with whitecaps.

'Sea State 5,' Major Jinko said to Ben, mouthing the words so that he could be understood above the increased engine noise now that the ramp was down.

Ben nodded and gave a thumbs up. Dropping to one knee beside Caesar, he pulled his partner in close.

'We can handle Sea State 5, can't we, mate? And we're ready for a swim.'

Caesar's response was a lick on the cheek. At the mention of the word 'swim', the labrador's tail had begun to wag furiously. After parachute jumps – especially freefall parachute jumps that sent the slipstream rapidly coursing over his nose – Caesar loved swimming the most. Like all labradors, his slightly webbed feet made him a strong swimmer. But it was the fun of being in the water that excited him. Yet he hated bath time! Taking a bath was not Caesar's idea of a water sport.

Just a few metres from Ben and Caesar, Charlie was talking into an intercom headset connected to the fuselage by a long black cable. Despite the fact that Major Jinko outranked him, it was Charlie, as on-the-ground team leader for Operation Pink Elephant, who was in charge of the jump. And he wanted to satisfy himself that the pilot knew what she was doing. Life and limb were at risk in a hazardous jump such as this one. 'Wind speed and direction, please, ma'am?' he asked Squadron Leader O'Shay.

'Wind south by southwest, thirty-five knots,' the pilot immediately replied from the flight deck. 'Rely on me to get you onto the flat-top, Sergeant. I have done this once or twice before, you know.'

Charlie smiled. 'Roger to that, ma'am.'

'Commencing first run in sixty seconds,' said O'Shay. 'Seven minutes to green light.'

'Copy that. Seven minutes.'

'Good luck with your mission.'

'Thanks for the ride, ma'am.' Removing the headset, Charlie pulled on his Kevlar combat helmet. Once he'd tightened the strap under his chin, he moved toward the rear of the aircraft and the open tailgate.

Five men hand-picked by Charlie were waiting in line. Charlie now took his place at the head of the line. He would be leading the first group to jump. Turning to the men behind him, he raised seven gloved fingers to indicate it would be seven minutes until the jump. Then, raising his eyes, he locked his gaze on a red light glowing on the fuselage wall beside the open tail. The remaining members of the team, those who weren't jumping this time, stood back and waited their turn. Six of them would be jumping on the second pass over *Canberra*, and Ben and Caesar on the last pass.

The Hercules had been losing altitude for several minutes. It now levelled out at 1000 feet and flew into the wind. The pilot throttled back until the plane seemed to creep over the ocean. The minutes passed. And then *Canberra*'s bulk was passing below the plane. In that instant, the red light on the fuselage wall turned to green. As one, Charlie and his group ran along the ramp and jumped out into midair. Baz came immediately behind Charlie, then Bruce, Banner, Mortenson and Major Jinko. Moments after each man jumped, he pulled his ripcord. Soon it was possible for those remaining inside the Hercules' vast cargo cabin to see six deployed chutes floating back toward *Canberra* in neat single file, each one a little lower than the next. Carried by the wind, and guided by each parachutist, the rectangular chutes sank slowly and precisely toward the ship.

The Hercules' engines began to roar loudly as the pilot applied more power. The plane's nose came up and the Herc began to climb, banking gently to the left. The aircraft was gaining height and commencing a long circular flight path, ready for run number two. Sergeant Duke Hazard was now talking to the pilot via the intercom. Leading the second group, he waited until Squadron Leader O'Shay told him that the green light was just minutes away, then joined his group as they formed a line by the open tail. Coming down to 1000 feet once more and levelling out, the Hercules again flew a course that put *Canberra* directly ahead.

The first six parachutists dropped toward the *Canberra*'s deck, which had looked worryingly small from the air. But as the GRRR team members got closer, it began to look the size of a football field. All six men were highly experienced parachutists and, guiding their chutes with control lines in each hand, they were able to steer them as if they were gliders.

Even so, their speed and the ship's momentum in the opposite direction meant that their landings would be swift. To counter this, Charlie and those following him executed a tight manoeuvre. They steered their chutes to the right of the fast-approaching ship, then made a rapid left-hand turn and came in from the side, partially into the wind, so that they landed going in much the same direction as the ship and at little more than *Canberra*'s speed. Only hugely experienced jumpers could pull off a landing like this – precise and without injury.

Charlie touched down first, slap-bang in the middle of the flight deck. His carbon-fibre Zoomers had a little give in them – but more give than human legs – and he was able to land on the deck and run along it for several metres with an almost bouncy gait until, still on his feet and letting the air out of his chute, he came to a stand-still. Most of the others, including Major Jinko, made similarly perfect touchdowns.

Casper Mortenson was the exception, losing his balance and falling to the steel deck, where he was dragged along for some distance until he smacked the emergency release in the middle of his chest. The harness immediately came away, releasing the Dane from his parachute. It caught the strong breeze, billowed and blew over the edge of the flight deck, dropping into the ocean.

With the size of the swells, no boat could be launched from the *Canberra* to recover the lost chute. And the helicopter hovering behind the ship could not afford to divert from its paramount mission of being ready to zoom in and lower a line to any jumper unlucky enough to miss his flight deck landing and go over the ship's side. The chute would float in the ocean until it was washed up on some distant shore, where locals might treasure this silken bounty from the sea.

'Untidy, Casper,' Charlie called over to the Dane, as he reeled in his deflated chute.

Mortenson shrugged. 'I'm a better diver than I am a parachutist,' he retorted.

Canberra sailors now appeared, running across the deck to help the parachutists free themselves from their chutes. They then led each man to the 'island', the tall section of the ship's superstructure that rose on the starboard side like a grey office tower. Via the island, they would enter the bowels of the ship.

The deck officer looked down at the scene from the bridge. 'First party of parachutists recovered, Captain.'

'Very good,' said Captain Rixon. 'So far, so good.'

'Sea State 5 edging into Sea State 6, Captain,' the navigation officer warned, reading the data from a screen in front of him.

'Do we recall the heelo, sir?' the air division commander asked anxiously. 'And tell Blue Orchid to abort its remaining passes?'

Rising from his chair, Captain Rixon walked to the bridge window and studied his ship's flight deck. A little up-and-down motion was visible as the ship pushed its way into the increasingly larger swells, but in Rixon's opinion the Seahawk should be able to land in such conditions with comparative ease. His new ship was performing above expectations. 'No,' he said firmly. 'Prepare to receive the next airdrop.'

From inside the Hercules, Ben and Caesar watched as Duke Hazard led the second GRRR group out the back of the plane. McHenry, Cisco, Harada, Lyon and Wolf followed right behind the American Green Beret. Once again the Hercules climbed after the jumpers had exited, then came around for its third pass over the LHD.

The C-130's loadmaster now came to Ben, who was kneeling to fit Caesar's doggles. 'Good to go, Sergeant?' yelled the loadmaster.

Ben nodded and stood up. 'Yep. Let's do it.'

The loadmaster picked up Caesar and held him up against Ben. The loadmaster had flown with EDDs before and knew exactly what was required when an

EDD and its handler made a parachute jump. The labrador wore a jumping harness made especially for war dogs, and Ben now clipped this to his own harness. As the loadmaster let go of the labrador and stepped back, Caesar was left hanging sideways across Ben's stomach. The arrangement looked inelegant, and Caesar appeared out of his comfort zone, but it was the only way that he and Ben could jump together.

Ben ruffled the labrador's ears. 'We'll soon be in the water and having a lovely swim, mate.'

Caesar's tail wagged, but not as enthusiastically as before. He had a look on his face that seemed to say, *Let's just get on with it, boss!*

Laden with Caesar, parachute and equipment packs, Ben moved to the open rear of the plane and stood with his eye on the signal lamp on the wall, which had been glowing red since the second GRRR group jumped. The loadmaster spoke to the pilot via his headset, then held up two fingers – two minutes to go. Before long, *Canberra* was passing below, smaller than it had appeared on the two previous passes, because the Hercules was making this final run at the higher altitude of 2000 feet.

The light turned green. Ben waddled forward and dropped from the end of the ramp. The moment he cleared the aircraft, he pulled his ripcord. The small pilot chute shot up, dragging the main chute with it. Within seconds, Ben and Caesar's rapid fall was checked, as the main chute opened. Ben grasped the toggles at the end of two lines dangling from the deployed parachute and tugged gently on the one on the right. The parachute angled in that direction, and man and dog turned to the south of the approaching *Canberra*. The ship's flight deck had by this time been cleared of the six jumpers from the second pass; all had landed without incident. Now it was just a matter of recovering Ben and Caesar to complete the warship's reception of the GRRR team.

Ben didn't have to be as accurate as the first twelve jumpers. All he had to do was land in the sea 300–400 metres off the ship's port side. The lower the pair descended, the rougher the sea began to appear – and the higher the swells. To slow their impact with the water, Ben followed the example of the previous jumpers, angling his chute in a shallow turn to his left, toward the ship, so that they were almost into the wind.

'Here we go, Caesar!' Ben called, as the surface of the water rushed to meet them.

Ben entered the water feet first. Their combined weight plus the speed of their fall meant that he and Caesar were plunged under the waves and disappeared from view. Ben's parachute crumpled on the surface of the water. His lifejacket deployed automatically with a *whoosh*! Within seconds, the inflated jacket propelled them upwards. As soon as Ben's head broke the surface, he leaned back so that Caesar's head was also above water. Methodically,

Ben punched the parachute release, and he and Caesar were instantly freed of the dragging chute.

Much like Casper Mortenson's chute, this one would also remain in the sea. In his head, Ben could hear Josh and Maddie scolding him for littering the Indian Ocean. But he knew that the parachute would end up making someone's day. He had seen such discarded chutes used by villagers in the Maldive Islands to make tents, or to make dresses for the poor in Bangladesh. One man's loss was another man's gain, he told himself. Besides, this mission was all about saving lives.

Normally in a jump into water, Ben would promptly disengage the clip that held Caesar to his torso, and Caesar would slip off him and begin paddling at his side. But for what lay ahead, man and dog needed to remain attached.

'Won't be long, mate,' Ben assured his partner.

Ben tried to spot the ship but the rolling waves, now more than four metres high, blocked it from his view. Water washed over the pair of them in sheets. It covered Caesar entirely for long seconds and filled Ben's mouth, leaving him coughing and spluttering. In trying to keep Caesar's head above water, Ben was leaning back so far that he was regularly receiving a ducking and gasping for air. They couldn't stay in such rough water for much longer. Both man and dog could drown.

Ben reached for his lifejacket and freed a flare from

its clip. Yanking on one end of the flare, he set it off. An orange light burned bright as he held the flare aloft, its orange smoke trailing away on the strong breeze. The flare was impervious to the water that continued to wash over Ben and Caesar; nothing would put it out until the flare ran out. After just a few minutes, a hulking shape appeared just twenty metres above the pair. Attracted by the flare, *Canberra*'s ASR Seahawk had arrived.

From the heelo's right side, a wire was winched down. There was a basic harness at the end of the wire, and once this reached the water's surface, the Seahawk's pilot manoeuvred his hovering machine until the harness was within Ben's reach. Ben expertly hooked the harness under both his arms, then gave a thumbs up to the winchman leaning out of the helicopter. The electric winch began to turn, and Ben and Caesar were lifted from the water just as a wave crashed over them. Dripping wet, the pair was hauled up to the Seahawk's open rear compartment. The winchman dragged them in, and soon Ben and Caesar were sitting on the heelo's floor.

'Recovery complete, skip,' the winchman informed his pilot over the intercom.

'Roger,' the pilot responded.

The Seahawk rose and turned, banking around toward *Canberra*, which was now some distance ahead. Rapidly, the chopper overhauled the ship and approached it from astern until it was hovering ten metres above the deck of the moving vessel. On the side of the flight deck, a navy batman in helmet and iridescent jacket waved his bats to guide the pilot in. The pilot, unable to see directly beneath his aircraft, had to rely on the batman for directions. Down the Seahawk slowly came, until its wheels touched the deck. The machine bounced back up into the air slightly, then settled firmly on the steel, and the batman signalled that the heelo was down. Only now did Ben unclip Caesar from his harness.

All around the heelo, members of the ship's deck team were appearing – men in helmets whose vests of different colours signified their departments, from fuel to armaments to maintenance. They quickly took charge of the helicopter from the aircrew.

Above the whine of the dying engines, one of the deck crew yelled to Ben, 'Need a hand, mate?'

'No, thanks,' Ben replied, jumping down to the deck. Turning back to the helicopter's cabin, he saw Caesar standing on the edge, looking down at the deck and assessing this strange new environment.

'Come on, Caesar,' Ben called. 'It's fine. Down you come.'

Trusting Ben implicitly, Caesar jumped down. One of the deck crew, a big smile on his face, went to give Caesar a pat.

'Hold on,' Ben cautioned him.

As the sailor, frowning, looked up at Ben questioningly, Caesar shook himself vigorously from head to tail. The sailors nearest him received a spray of water, bringing laughs from their companions. Ben smiled – he'd known what was coming. Clipping Caesar's two-metre galvanised steel leash in place, he looked at the crew chief. 'Okay, where to?'

'Follow this man,' the crew chief replied, patting the back of the sailor beside him.

The seaman led Ben and Caesar across the deck, the labrador trotting along beside his handler with his nose to the steel, sniffing it out.

A chief petty officer met Ben at a door to the island. 'Welcome aboard *Canberra*, Sergeant,' said the CPO, shaking Ben's hand. 'Good to have you aboard.'

'Thanks,' said Ben. 'Good to be aboard.'

Before following the CPO into the ship's interior, Ben turned and looked back at the helicopter. The three-man flight crew were walking his way while the deck crew folded the helicopter's tail to one side and manhandled the machine toward a large aircraft lift in the stern. Spray was regularly coming over the ship's bow, and with each big wave that hit, the deck juddered. Ben reckoned the wind had picked up since he'd jumped.

'Still Sea State 5?' he asked the CPO.

The CPO smiled wryly. 'It's increased to Sea State 6,' he said. 'You were lucky the captain decided to keep the heelo aloft, mate. Otherwise, you and your dog would be swimming to Africa!'

Nearby, a rooster crowed. Lucky Mertz jerked awake. Flies were crawling around the corners of his eyes, trying to get into them. With a curse, he swatted them away. Lucky had always wondered why flies were so attracted to human eyes. He leaned against the wall and placed his akubra over his face in an attempt to keep the flies away.

But the hat could not keep out the smell in the hut. Their captors had given the prisoners a single plastic bucket to use as their lavatory, only emptying it once a day. And several of the captives had developed diarrhoea from their diet of bean soup and green bananas. It was no wonder the hut was full of flies.

Lucky had slept sitting upright, his arms tied in front of him at the wrists. He looked around the gloomy hut interior at his five companions, all of them native rangers from the Tanzanian Wildlife Service. Lucky hadn't been working with them long, but had quickly grown to know and like each one.

Julius, the oldest, grey-haired and in his sixties, was the senior man among them. He had been a ranger for many years, ever since the poaching of elephants had been made illegal in 1989. Three of the others, Simel, Nelson and Roadga, were young men in their twenties, each with a few years of ranger service under his belt. And then there was Koinet – or 'the tall one', as the local people called him. Just sixteen years of age, he had only been a ranger for several months.

Young Koinet was finding captivity by the rebels harder to take than the older rangers. He had seen nothing of the world outside the bush, and his biggest dream was of one day visiting Dar es Salaam, the largest city of Tanzania. Koinet had confessed to Lucky after their capture by RAT that he had only joined the ranger service to get the fine pair of military boots that came with the job – boots that had been confiscated by the rebels after his capture. He'd had no desire to protect animals or to get into battles with poachers. Koinet was pining for his mother and regretting ever putting on his ranger boots. As the others around him sat up, stretching and yawning, Koinet lay curled up like a lazy kitten.

Chickens outside the hut scattered with much frantic clucking before the hut door swung open. Two rebels in jeans and T-shirts entered, each holding an AK-47 assault rifle. Heedlessly treading on legs and feet to get to Lucky, they grasped him under the arms and dragged him from the group. His hat went flying as they pulled him out the door.

'What's going on?' Lucky demanded. 'Where are you taking me?'

The pair remained mute. They merely threw him in the dirt full-length. Looking up, Lucky saw a short man with unusually pale skin approaching. A holstered automatic pistol was suspended from his belt, and a pair of binoculars hung from his neck. He wore green camouflage military-style trousers, and a red beret sat atop his curly white hair. Thick dark glasses covered his eyes.

'Good morning, Ranger Lucky,' said the man, folding his arms as he looked down at him.

'Good morning, Colonel.' Lucky struggled to his feet and found himself towering a good six inches above the man. This was Abraham Zuba – or Colonel Pink Eye, as the locals called him – Commander of the Revolutionary Army of Tanzania. After Julius and the other rangers had been captured by Zuba's men, Lucky had tried to negotiate with Zuba for their release. Instead, Zuba had threatened to execute Koinet unless Lucky surrendered himself to the rebels. To emphasise his point, Zuba had fired a pistol beside Koinet's right ear – Koinet had been deaf in that ear for days after. And so Lucky had voluntarily become a prisoner of the elephant poachers.

Zuba turned and walked away. 'Come, I have something to show you, Ranger Lucky,' he called.

Seeing Lucky hesitate, one of the rebel soldiers jabbed him in the middle of the back with the butt of his AK-47, propelling him forward. Lucky stumbled after Zuba, and the two soldiers followed close behind. They came to a clear area in the middle of the village of thirty huts. Most of the huts were like the one where Lucky and the other prisoners were being kept – round, with mud walls and roofs of thatch. One or two of the administrative buildings, such as the village school, were rectangular and roofed with rusty corrugated iron. Beyond the huts were a number of compounds with walls made from tree branches. They reached the height of the shoulders of an average local. Some of these compounds housed the villagers' goats. Bony cattle, the night-time inmates of other compounds, were currently grazing contentedly on the outskirts of the village.

A number of fearful villagers hung back, watching from a distance as more of Zuba's armed soldiers assembled. Lucky estimated there were about twenty of these soldiers. Most were only boys in their teens – short and malnourished, with empty eyes. Some wore boots, including those taken from the rangers. Lucky, who was tall and rangy, had such big feet that no African could fit into his boots, so he'd been permitted to keep his footwear. The other boy soldiers were barefoot, yet most of them carried AK-47s. In this part of the world it was easier to lay your hands on an assault rifle than it was to get a pair of shoes.

Lucky also noted that one soldier was armed with a rocket-propelled grenade launcher – an RPG – and another had a large Russian machinegun slung across his chest. These poachers were more heavily armed than a typical Tanzanian Army patrol and certainly more heavily armed than rangers of the Tanzanian Wildlife Service.

The boy soldiers were being supervised by a lithe man with a grey beard. He wore blue shorts and, like Zuba, he had on a pair of military-style boots, a red beret and a camouflage jacket. He carried a pump-action shotgun, had a large radio strapped on his back, and there was a large sheathed machete hanging from his belt. Zuba's soldiers were busy mustering a group of frightened-looking boys. Lucky guessed that they were from the local district and had been rounded up by Zuba's so-called soldiers.

'See here, Ranger Lucky,' said Zuba, beckoning to him with a sly smile.

Receiving another jab from behind, Lucky moved toward the rebel leader.

'These are my new recruits,' Zuba told Lucky. 'Captain Chawinga, give me your machete.'

'Yes, Colonel.' The grey-bearded man in the red beret slid his machete from its scabbard and handed it to his commander.

The two soldiers who had taken Lucky from the hut

each clamped a hand on his shoulders, holding him firmly in place. Smiling all the while, Zuba strolled along the ragged line of boys, some of whom Lucky estimated were only eight or nine years of age. Zuba stopped in front of the shortest boy, whose only clothing was a pair of grubby white shorts, and lay the flat of the machete blade on the youth's bare right shoulder. 'You, boy. Do you know who I am?'

The boy began to shake with fear. Too frightened to speak, he could only nod in reply. His eyes strayed to the sharp blade perilously close to his neck.

'Of course you know who I am,' Zuba said with a laugh. 'Who in this country does not know of Colonel Zuba and the mighty Revolutionary Army of Tanzania? Would you like to be a member of my brave army, boy, and liberate your country from injustice and corruption? Hmm?'

The boy said nothing. He couldn't lift his eyes from the machete.

Zuba scowled. 'You *do* wish to serve in my army, don't you, boy?'

The boy's gaze flashed to Zuba, then to the machete. He nodded vigorously.

The smile returned to Zuba's face. 'Good. Very good. Wise boy, clever boy. What do they call you?' When the boy failed to answer, he added menacingly, 'Speak up!'

'S-s-sironka,' the boy stammered softly.

'Sironka? You know what that means, don't you? You are "the pure one". I have another Sironka in my ranks. He is not pure. Are you pure, boy?'

Sironka didn't reply.

'Very well, pure one, let us see if you meet the basic qualification for membership of my army.' Zuba took a step back. 'Come forward,' he commanded, pointing to the ground with the machete.

Warily, the boy did as he'd been bidden.

'Chawinga, put him to the test,' Zuba instructed.

'Yes, Colonel.' Chawinga in turn pointed to one of their soldiers. 'Do it!' he growled. The boy soldier in question scuttled to the terrified child then knelt beside him.

'Zuba, what are you doing?' Lucky called.

Zuba turned to Lucky and his smile widened. 'You will see.'

The boy soldier took up his AK-47, stood the butt on the ground and then put his fingers on the end of the barrel. The gun stood upright beside Sironka.

'What do you think, Chawinga?' Zuba asked. 'Is he tall enough?'

Chawinga came and took a closer look, then shook his head. 'No, Colonel. This fish is too small. Throw it back.'

Zuba chuckled at the youth. 'Unfortunately, boy, you have not passed the test. To be one of my soldiers, you must be longer than a Kalashnikov rifle. This is my rule. So, Sironka, you may return to your home. Next year you will be longer than a Kalashnikov, that I guarantee. And then we shall meet again. Go, pure one. Run home to your mother!' He waved the machete in the direction of the surrounding farmland.

Sironka looked at the rifle beside him, then at Zuba, then at Chawinga.

'Run, the colonel say!' Chawinga growled. 'Go!'

With that, the boy took off, running from the village as fast as his legs would carry him. The sight brought laughter from Zuba, with his boy soldiers following his cue and doing the same.

Lucky could do nothing but watch as potential recruits were put to the Kalashnikov test, and the remainder all passed. Zuba now had seven fresh recruits. As he handed the machete back to Chawinga, an elderly man in the crowd of villagers came forward and spoke anxiously to Zuba in the local dialect. The rebel commander looked him up and down, then waved him away. When the old man protested, Chawinga and another soldier grabbed his arms and frogmarched him away.

'Ranger Lucky,' said Zuba, pointing at him. 'You will come with me. We shall walk and talk.'

Lucky joined the colonel, and together, prisoner and captor walked from the village and out onto the flat, dry earth surrounding it. They followed a dusty track with bananas growing on either side of it. 'What did the old villager say to you?' Lucky asked, glancing over his shoulder to see two armed guards shadowing them.

'His grandson is one of today's new recruits,' Zuba replied. 'This grandfather, he offered to take the boy's place in the ranks of my army. But children obey orders, old men do not.' He smiled. 'Old men have consciences. Children are too young and inexperienced to even know what a conscience is. Children can be moulded like dough. Old men cannot, they have already been in the oven of life. They are like old bread – hard and stale.'

'It's cynical and cruel to make soldiers of children.'

Zuba shrugged. 'Life is cruel. This way, a boy becomes a man very quickly. I am doing them all a favour.'

Deciding that he would get nowhere arguing with the rebel leader, Lucky changed the subject. 'What do you plan to do with me and my men, Colonel?'

'Your men I do not care about, but *you* are a valuable commodity, Ranger Lucky,' Zuba replied. 'Perhaps we shall trade you to the government.'

'Trade me for what?'

'Perhaps for a promise from the government not to bother us anymore.'

'That won't happen,' said Lucky. 'The Tanzanian Government is committed to stamping out poaching. More and more foreign aid to Tanzania from countries like the US, Britain and Australia is being linked to that commitment. If they want the aid to continue, they can't afford to let you continue poaching elephants.'

'You underestimate your value, Ranger Lucky.' Coming to a halt under the shade of a flame tree, Zuba put one boot on a boulder and looked out over the plain. 'Your capture tells the government that it is useless to oppose my men and myself. Look at you, a foreign mercenary, a Special Forces soldier sent to train their rangers to fight us. Within a month of your arrival in my country, I capture you! What does that say? It says that I am much too clever for those fools in the government. And they know it!'

'I won't be the last foreigner who comes to this country to oppose you.'

Zuba glared at Lucky. 'You *mzungu* think you know everything!' he snapped. 'But you do not know this country, you do not know its people. The British colonised this country, yet they never understood it. They did not *want* to understand it.'

Lucky had learned that *mzungu* was a Tanzanian word that meant white people. 'And you do understand Tanzania and its people?' he asked scornfully.

Zuba's smile returned. 'Precisely. To the people of Tanzania, I am a hero. The people love me.'

'And what happens when you have butchered every elephant in Tanzania? Will you be a hero then?'

'Pah!' Zuba waved the machete in the air. 'There will always be elephants in this country.'

'Not at the rate you're killing them. If you are a hero, you should have no need to kill elephants for their ivory to finance your "army".'

'Farmers kill elephants that trample their crops,' Zuba countered, still looking out at the landscape as the sun rose higher in the early morning sky. 'The government takes money from game hunters to let them shoot elephants.' He turned to Lucky. 'Do you know how much they charge those white hunters for a twenty-eight-day elephant hunting licence, Ranger Lucky? I will tell you – twenty-five thousand dollars. These big brave game hunters are only interested in having their photographs taken with the animals they shoot. And yet they say my men and I are criminals if we kill just one elephant for its tusks and a noble cause!'

'I'm not in favour of killing a single elephant. But the game hunters only shoot a hundred elephants per year. *You* are killing tens of thousands!'

'My army needs much money to wage war against oppression,' Zuba said matter-of-factly.

Lucky shook his head. 'You shouldn't need an army. If the people love you, as you say, they would elect you their leader.'

'Elect me?' Zuba threw his head back and laughed uproariously. When he looked at Lucky again, the expression on his face was serious once more. 'They would not permit me to stand for election. Look at me, *mzungu*!' He pulled off his sunglasses to reveal eyes pink-purple in colour. 'I am an albino! Do you know what that means?'

'It means your skin pigmentation is lighter than usual and you are affected by bright light –'

'Not the clinical definition!' Zuba snapped, returning the glasses to his eyes. 'It means that I am an outcast in my own land! When I was a child, the government would not permit me to attend school. They said I would scare the other children and put them off their learning. After my mother died, my father tried to give me to an orphanage, but the white church people threw me out after I was laughed at, spat on and beaten by the other children for being different. The whites said I caused friction among the other orphans. So, I have been an outcast ever since. Even the dogs bark at an albino child. They, too, knew I was different.'

Lucky felt a genuine pity for the man. 'I'm sorry to hear that.'

'I do not seek your pity,' Zuba said coldly. 'I do not need pity. As a boy, no one wanted me or gave me a chance. I had to fend for myself. Did you know, in Tanzania, witchcraft is still practised to this day? And there is a myth here that the bones of albino children make powerful potions. Sometimes, the bones of albino children have been sold to witches, who grind them up to make their potions. It still occurs to this very day.'

'People here don't still believe in witches, do they?' Lucky asked, incredulous. 'Not in this modern age.'

Zuba smiled wistfully. 'There is nothing modern about life in the African bush, my friend. Here, life is as primitive as it has been for thousands of years. And they still believe in witches. When I was a child, three men kidnapped me. I overheard them talking about selling my body to a witch for many thousands of dollars. But I broke free and was able to grab one of their rifles. I shot and wounded all three of my captors.'

'And you escaped?'

Zuba nodded. 'That episode taught me a valuable lesson.' Reaching to the holster on his hip, he withdrew a Glock semi-automatic pistol. 'I learned that the man with the gun is the one who receives respect in this world. And any man who laughs at me – any dog that barks at me – I shoot him! No one argues with Abraham Zuba now, I can tell you. Now they respect me and do as I tell them.'

'Is it respect that makes people do as you tell them, or fear?' said Lucky.

Zuba's smile returned. 'Yes, they respect me. But first they must fear me. Do *you* fear me, Ranger Lucky?'

Lucky shook his head. 'No.'

Zuba could see that Lucky was telling the truth.

'Do you know, I think you are either a very brave man or a very great fool.'

They were interrupted by Chawinga jogging toward them. 'Colonel, Mboko has been on the radio,' he called. 'He says we must move! Military vehicles are approaching.'

Zuba slid the pistol back into its holster. 'Then move, we shall,' he declared. 'Get everything ready, Chawinga. We pull out of Leboo at once. We will head north, to the lake. But to put off villagers with big eyes and even bigger tongues, we will begin by heading west.'

'Yes, Colonel.' Chawinga turned and headed off to order preparations for their departure.

By the time Lucky had walked back to the village with Zuba and his two guards, it was enveloped in yellow dust stirred by the urgent activity. Two old green Land Rovers and a score of dusty trail bikes had been brought out of their camouflaged hiding places. As they approached, the village headman came toward Zuba with his hand outstretched. Zuba and the headman argued briefly in the local dialect before Zuba roughly pushed him away, leaving the man to glare at him with hate in his eyes.

'What did he want?' Lucky asked.

'This headman invited my soldiers and myself to his village in the expectation that I would give him American dollars, as I usually do,' Zuba explained. 'But until I receive the cash from the last shipment of ivory, my army and myself have no American dollars for this man or for anyone else. Now, rejoin your men, Ranger Lucky.' He pointed to the nearest Land Rover. 'We will speak again later.'

With that, Lucky was hustled away by the two guards. He and his rangers were pushed into the back of one Land Rover, the new boy recruits into the other, as Zuba's soldiers mounted the trail bikes, some with a pair of riders. One of Zuba's older recruits came running with a bleating goat draped around his neck. With a grin, the thief took a seat on the back of one of the trail bikes and clasped the goat's hoofs together on his chest. He would ride by holding on with his knees. Zuba climbed into the front Land Rover. Chawinga mounted the running board of the other. Standing there and holding on with one hand, he pointed west with his shotgun, and the vehicles moved off.

Crammed together in the back of the Land Rover, the five captive rangers looked at Lucky.

'What are they going to do with us, boss?' asked Koinet.

'They're taking us to a new location,' Lucky advised. 'The Tanzanian Army is close by.'

'Ah,' said old Julius, sounding hopeful. 'The army will save us.'

'No, they will not,' Koinet moaned. 'The army fears Colonel Pink Eye. They have never caught him. We are doomed!'

'No, we're not doomed,' Lucky assured him, lowering his voice and beckoning the others to lean in closer. 'One of two things is going to happen to us – either the authorities will pay for our release, or Special Forces troops will free us.'

This lit up the faces of all but Koinet. 'What Special Forces troops?' he demanded. 'The Tanzanian Army has no Special Forces.'

'No, but the United Nations does,' Lucky countered.

'Why would the UN send Special Forces to free us, of all people?' Koinet demanded.

Lucky, a former GRRR operative, had sworn an oath of secrecy about the GRRR and its operations. But he had a sneaking suspicion that Secretary-General Park might send his former comrades to rescue him. Not that he thought himself special. Lucky just knew the UN looked after its own, and he suspected that his plight had not gone unnoticed at UN headquarters. 'Trust me and don't lose hope,' he said. 'One way or another, we're all going to get out of this just fine.'

'Yes, Ranger Lucky,' said Julius, smiling. 'Just fine.'

But Koinet did not smile.

In a cloud of dust, the convoy departed Leboo. With Land Rover motors straining and bike engines buzzing like angry wasps, the convoy bumped away toward the west. The villagers watched them go and spoke urgently among themselves. Zuba was right not to trust these locals. The greedy headman and several of his villagers who had lost sons to Zuba's army would be keen to tell government troops the direction which the RAT vehicles had taken. Anticipating this, Zuba would order a sharp change of direction once the convoy was well out of sight and sound of the villagers.

As he was bounced around the rear of the Land Rover, Lucky considered that, if the authorities didn't pay a ransom for them or the GRRR didn't launch a rescue, he would have to turn to a third option. He might have to employ his own Special Forces skills to save his rangers and himself. But that was a risky option which could result in the endangerment of his men. It was an option he would only consider as a last resort.

CHAPTER 8

Ben and Caesar had been escorted down to *Canberra*'s accommodation deck, between the hangar deck above, where the ship's aircraft were stored, and the well deck below, which housed *Canberra*'s landing craft. The accommodation deck contained quarters for the ship's crew plus up to 2000 troops when the ship was involved in a landing operation. There were large messes down here and a hospital with sixty beds. This was a floating city.

'We've improvised quarters for your EDD on the well deck,' the CPO told Ben, as he led him to a long room full of bunks. Here, other GRRR men were already unloading their equipment.

'What sort of quarters?' Ben asked.

'A cage of sorts.'

Ben shook his head. 'No cages. We won't be aboard long. Caesar will stay with me.'

'That's right,' said Baz. He was lying on a nearby bunk with his hands locked behind his head. 'Caesar is one of us.'

'Suit yourself,' the CPO replied. 'Find a bunk, Sergeant, stow your gear and lighten your load.' He then turned on his heel and left Ben to it.

Ben patted the mattress of an empty bunk, and Caesar happily jumped up on it and lay full-length. With his tongue hanging out, Caesar watched Ben check the contents of his equipment bags. Caesar was happy as long as he was with Ben. The pair had been high in the clouds making HALO parachute jumps, in the back of Bushmasters under enemy fire, and under water in a cramped submarine. Yet, in every situation the labrador was always calm and ready to follow Ben's instructions without hesitation. He trusted Ben implicitly, just as Ben trusted him with his life.

'Get a bit wet, mate?' said Charlie, coming to give Caesar a pat.

Caesar licked his hand in response and wagged his tail.

'The swells out there were massive,' said Ben. Looking around, he noticed that Major Jinko was missing. 'Where's the bear?'

'Upstairs, getting a briefing from the ship's captain.'

'I think you'll find that it's actually "aloft" on a ship, Charlie, not "upstairs",' said Baz, sitting up and dangling his feet over the side of his bunk.

'Same difference,' Charlie returned good-naturedly.

Meanwhile, aloft in *Canberra*'s operations centre located in the island, Major Jinko was meeting with Captain Rixon and Air Division Commander Lockhart. The operations centre was a long, narrow windowless room bathed in a dull blue light. It was lined with dozens of operators sitting in front of keyboards, control panels and large LCD screens which spookily lit up their faces. From this room, all air, land and sea operations mounted from *Canberra* were controlled by Navy, Army and Air Force personnel.

Jinko joined the two senior naval officers standing behind the screens of two RAAF operators. Those screens displayed a variety of images of the ocean, taken from high in the sky. One of the operators was manipulating a joystick.

'Not very interesting pictures at present, I'll admit,' said Lockhart.

'Where are they coming from?' asked Jinko.

'From a Bluey out over the waters between Tanzania and Zanzibar, at 32,000 feet.'

'And a Bluey is . . .?'

'A drone, a Heron UAV from the RAAF's Number 5 Flight,' the naval officer replied. 'The RAAF have given their Herons the nickname "Blueys". Those babies have a 16.6-metre wingspan – almost the size of a regular fighter aircraft.'

Jinko nodded. 'I know about Herons. We used them to support special ops in Afghanistan. So, what was this particular Heron doing aboard *Canberra*?'

'We've been evaluating it for maritime cooperation use,' Captain Rixon replied.

'It was launched twenty-eight hours ago,' said the air division commander. 'But the weather has been so dirty down here we haven't been able to land it again. We'll have to keep it up there above the clouds until the weather clears.'

'How long can it stay up for?' Jinko asked, studying the two RAAF men in charge of the Heron. The operator using the joystick had an array of flying instruments in front of him. He was the UAV's pilot and was actually flying the distant plane. The other man was in charge of the cameras and sensors aboard the Heron. If the aircraft had been armed with missiles, this man would also have had control of them, aiming, firing and directing them from his desk.

'The Bluey carries enough fuel to stay aloft for fifty-two hours,' said Lockhart.

Jinko gave a low whistle. 'Impressive. And you think it can play a role in Operation Pink Elephant, Captain?'

'SOCOM thinks it can,' Rixon replied. 'We can position the Heron in the air above the area of operations, to let you and SOCOM see what's happening on the ground.'

'Our eye in the sky,' said Jinko. 'I like it. But you've first got to get it safely back aboard. Am I right?'

'We will,' Rixon said confidently. 'The weather is forecast to clear overnight.' He turned and walked a few metres to a vacant seat at the long metal desk that ran the length of the narrow room. 'This will be your station for the operation, Major. You will control Operation Pink Elephant from this position.' He patted the desktop. 'And you'll have the Heron's operators right beside you.'

'Sounds good to me,' Jinko returned with a smile. 'What's the timeline?'

'We're currently steaming toward the Tanzanian coast to rendezvous with an escort vessel of the Tanzanian Navy. Once we're in position we'll be able to launch the heelos carrying your team, and the Heron. But we need to know where to send them. Does SOCOM have any idea where the rebels are holding the hostages at this time?'

'That, Captain Rixon, is the sixty-four million dollar question,' Jinko said with a sigh. 'Right now we don't have a clue where they are. But SOCOM is working on it with the Tanzanian Government.'

'Well, we can't very well launch a rescue mission until we know where your targets are.'

'Don't worry,' said Jinko, easing into the swivel chair that would be his for the duration of the operation. 'We'll get a lucky break on the intel before long. Our job is to be ready to act as soon as that happens.'

'We will,' Rixon said confidently. 'The weather is forecast to clear overnight.' He turned and walked a few metres to a vacant seat at the long metal desk that ran

As Captain Rixon had promised Major Jinko, the weather across the Indian Ocean had improved dramatically by the next morning.

Ben, who had slept in his bunk with Caesar lying beside him on top of the blanket, was up at the break of day with the rest of the GRRR team. After a shower and then breakfast in the ship's mess, Ben was ready for some exercise. While the other team members did press-ups and sit-ups in a corner of the flight deck, Ben took Caesar for a jog around the edge of the deck, which was the size of a football field. Unlike the previous day, the sky was a stunning clear blue and the ocean was a smooth Sea State 1. *Canberra* cruised along without the slightest movement of the deck.

As Ben and Caesar ran, they passed an angled section of the flight deck on the ship's port side which looked like a ski jump. In fact, that was what it was called and it was used to help launch fixed-wing aircraft into the air should the need arise. *Canberra* was officially only supposed to carry helicopters. One of those helicopters, a blue-grey Seahawk anti-submarine chopper, was on deck and preparing for take-off. Before long, with a roar from its noisy engines, it lifted into the air and buzzed away to the west.

Caesar, his tail wagging lazily, was enjoying the deck run. He took in the salty sea air and the faint aromas of sun-baked steel, aviation gasoline and the differing scents of the deck crew going about their daily duties. Caesar and Ben had completed two circuits of the deck and were near the stern when the ship began to turn into the wind. 'Clear the flight deck!' a voice blared over the loudspeakers. 'Prepare to recover UAV. Clear the flight deck! Prepare to recover UAV.'

A sailor popped up from beside the flight deck. 'You two can watch from down here,' he suggested, and Ben and Caesar jumped down to a platform a metre and a half below deck level, where deck crew were taking up positions. The friendly sailor pointed astern to a small black dot in the sky. 'There's the Heron.'

Ben watched as the dot grew larger. 'And the pilot of that thing is on board here somewhere?' he marvelled.

'He's sitting up in the operations room, looking at a bank of screens that are giving a pilot's eye view from cameras in the Heron,' the sailor replied. 'The marvels of modern technology, eh?'

Ben nodded. 'I'll say.'

As they watched, the elegant unmanned plane came angling down toward the deck, driven by a single propeller on its tail. As soon as its landing wheels touched deck, the engine went into reverse and revved madly, making a deafening racket. The Heron quickly ground to a halt and came to rest within a few metres of its touchdown point. Deck crew sprang from their watching places and ran to secure the UAV.

With the Heron soon being wheeled away to be taken down to the hangar deck, Ben and Caesar resumed their jog and completed a total of ten circuits by the time the Seahawk helicopter returned and landed. As the pair watched, a Tanzanian Navy officer stepped out from the chopper and was quickly escorted to the island. Ben squatted down and ruffled Caesar's neck. 'We can't be far from Tanzania now, mate,' he said. 'We'll soon be having some fun on dry land. Lots of interesting new smells for you where we're going.'

Caesar licked him on the cheek and then nuzzled playfully into his master. Caesar was ready to have some fun.

The Tanzanian officer was escorted up to the bridge, where he came to attention in front of Captain Rixon and gave a sloppy salute. 'Lieutenant Commander

Roadga Palla at your service, Captain,' he announced. 'I have the honour to captain the patrol vessel *Julius Nyere*, of the Tanzanian Navy's 701 Flotilla.'

Rixon returned Palla's salute, then reached out and shook his hand. 'Welcome aboard, Commander. You're with 701 Flotilla, you say? How many flotillas does the Tanzanian Navy possess?'

Lieutenant Commander Palla looked a little embarrassed. 'Just two, Captain. The other is a training flotilla.'

'Well, this joint operation with the Tanzanian Navy is a first for the Royal Australian Navy, Commander. We're pleased to be working with you.'

'Thank you, sir. My vessel is under orders to protect your ship at all costs, and I guarantee that it will do just that, sir, even if we go down fighting in the process!'

Rixon smiled. 'I don't imagine it will come to that, Commander. There are no maritime threats to *Canberra* in Tanzanian waters that I've been made aware of. Unless you have different information than I do?'

'Pirates, Captain,' Palla said earnestly.

Rixon raised an eyebrow. 'Pirates?'

'Somali pirates. Sudanese pirates.'

'This far south?'

Palla smiled weakly. 'One can never be too careful, sir.'

'We are always vigilant, Commander.'

'You can never be too vigilant, sir. At a distance, this

fine vessel of yours would look like a juicy container ship to pirates. Rely on my crew and myself to protect you with our very lives while you are in Tanzanian waters.'

A faint smile creased Rixon's lips. 'Very good. Carry on, Commander. My XO will brief you on our joint sailing plan.'

The pair exchanged salutes.

Within an hour, the Tanzanian patrol boat *Julius Nyere* had sped across the western horizon and joined *Canberra*. A tiny vessel in comparison to the Australian warship, and armed with a single small cannon in a forward turret, the patrol boat coursed along beside *Canberra* with most of its crew of thirty-five lounging on deck and watching as their skipper was returned to them by one of *Canberra's* inflatable boats.

Once Commander Palla was back aboard, the *Julius Nyere* pulled away and positioned itself 300 metres off *Canberra's* port side. The two vessels would continue in company this way, like a lion and her cub padding along together, until Operation Pink Elephant came to an end.

Summoned urgently, the members of the GRRR team quickly assembled in a briefing room deep inside *Canberra*. All with notepads on their laps, they settled in comfortable high-backed leather chairs normally occupied by aircrew receiving their flight briefings. The six crew members from two of the ship's Seahawk helicopters – all navy men – were also sitting in on the briefing, as were the two RAAF operators of the Heron UAV. Caesar lay at Ben's feet, contentedly gnawing a bone given to him by a navy cook.

Major Jinko stood at the front of the briefing room. 'This is the last known location we have for Zuba and the hostages,' he said, pointing to a map of Tanzania on a large screen. 'The intel is hot. At daybreak this morning they were in this village, Leboo, on the rim of the Kigosi Game Reserve in northwest Tanzania.'

A ripple of conversation ran around the room.

'Are they still there?' Charlie asked.

Jinko shook his head. 'No. They pulled out when a Tanzanian Army patrol got to within thirty clicks of them. According to locals, they headed west.'

'West?' said Tim McHenry. 'Where would that take them, Major?'

'My guess is, they're making a run for the border with Burundi,' Jinko replied, gesturing to the neighbouring country of Burundi on the map. 'They could reach it in a day. The Tanzanian military on the border has been alerted to be on the lookout for them.'

'How many men did Zuba have with him?' asked Jean-Claude Lyon.

'Around twenty, plus seven new recruits from the district – just kids, apparently.'

'Should be a piece of cake,' said Duke Hazard, half to himself. 'Once we locate 'em.'

Jinko then passed on another piece of information. 'The Tanzanian Government has today broadcast a statement announcing that it has dismissed Zuba's demands and called on him to set the hostages free.'

Tim McHenry scoffed. 'Like he'd do that!'

'It's now up to you people to get those hostages out of Zuba's hands,' Jinko declared.

'So, are we "go", sir?' Charlie asked.

'We are "go",' Jinko acknowledged with a faint smile.

'Yes!' Baz exclaimed, slapping his fist into the palm of his other hand. Baz and Lucky Mertz had been especially close during the years they had served together in the SAS. Both had come out of some pretty tough scrapes together, and they had always had each other's backs.

'Codenames are as follows,' Major Jinko advised, and each man prepared to write the details on his notepad. 'The ground team is Oscar Zulu. The heelos are Sally One and Sally Two. The Heron UAV is Bluey. Mission Control here aboard *Canberra* is Papa. *Canberra* is Mama. Lucky Mertz is Game Boy. The other hostages are Oasis. Colonel Zuba is Bullseye. Any questions?'

'How long do you figure we got to rescue Game Boy, Major?' Duke Hazard asked. 'Before Bullseye runs out of patience and lets his trigger finger do the talking for him?'

'SOCOM has had its psychoanalysts collate all the data they have on Zuba. Their assessment is that the man is a psychopath, but not stupid. He's cunning like a fox. He probably knows that his demands won't be met. Maybe he's just enjoying being able to call the shots for now. The man has an ego that would fill this room.'

'So, his patience will run out, or this all stops being fun for him, and he could start bumping off hostages?' said McHenry.

A grave expression came over Jinko's face. 'That is a possibility, yes.'

'So, I say again, sir,' Hazard called, 'how long do we have before he starts shooting?'

Jinko screwed up his face. 'Maybe forty-eight hours. Four or five days max. The man is unpredictable.'

Baz looked around at the other servicemen in the briefing room. 'Then let's do it, you blokes! There's no time to lose.'

CHAPTER 9

Josh dragged himself from the mat and stood, hunched, his white robes hanging loosely. His hands were raised and ready as he eyed off the larger boy who had just thrown him to the floor.

Josh had been taking unarmed combat lessons with Sergeant Brendan 'Iron Fist' Kasula at Holsworthy Barracks for a few months now. It was part of a deal that his dad had made with his school principal and the mother of Kelvin Corbett. Up till then, Kelvin had pushed Josh around, online and in person. Kelvin and his father had been jealous of all the attention that Josh had received because of Caesar. But bullies often meet their match, and Kelvin and his stepfather had met their match in Sergeant Ben Fulton.

Ben had thought Sergeant Kasula's lessons would be good for Josh as well as for Kelvin, but Josh hadn't been so sure. Kelvin was a year older than him, several inches taller and a lot heavier. Just the same, Josh had gone along to the lessons because his dad wanted him to.

Kelvin had had no choice after the school principal told his parents that he could be expelled if he failed to attend them.

Sergeant Kasula, also in loose white robes, stood between the pair. An Australian Army unarmed combat instructor, he was a massive, powerfully built man. He'd been born in Hawaii, and in his veins coursed the blood of the warrior chiefs of the Hawaiian Islands. Iron Fist Kasula could famously punch holes in a brick wall. He could also stand on one foot for a day without over-balancing. By his very size he was an intimidating figure. Yet, he had a surprisingly gentle nature when he was not practising martial arts.

'What did I tell you boys about size?' he asked Josh and Kelvin as they faced off for the tenth time this session.

'That size doesn't matter, Sergeant,' Josh replied, his eyes on Kelvin.

'And what did I tell you about weight?'

'You said that weight doesn't matter, Sergeant,' Kelvin replied.

'Very good. And what did I say was the most important thing of all?'

'Balance is the most important thing of all, Sergeant,' Josh and Kelvin replied together.

'Balance in *all* things, not just physical balance. Emotional balance. Balance in your diet. Balance in work and play. Balance in your opinion of your fellow man. What are other important qualities for a warrior?' He looked at Kelvin. 'Well?'

Kelvin pulled a pained face as he tried to remember the answer. 'I . . . I . . .'

'You knew the answer last week, Kelvin,' said the sergeant.

'Speed and agility,' Josh said in a low voice, trying to help Kelvin.

A broad smile lit up the instructor's face. 'Very good, young Fulton. You two are in this together. And by helping each other, you help yourself. This is one of the lessons that the warrior learns. It's called teamwork. But first you must learn to take care of yourselves as individuals.'

'My dad's a part of a team,' Josh said proudly. 'Dad, Caesar and Charlie.'

'Yes, they are, young Fulton,' Sergeant Kasula agreed. 'As individuals, balance, agility, speed and *concentration* – these are the qualities that will enable you to successfully take care of yourself, young Fulton. Until now, you have struggled to overcome a larger opponent. Let's see if you have taken on board the lessons I've been teaching you.' He took several paces back, then looked over at Kelvin. 'Ready?'

'Yes, Sergeant,' said Kelvin.

Kasula turned to Josh. 'Ready?'

Josh nodded. 'Yes, Sergeant.'

Over the past few months, Josh and Kelvin had attempted to put each other on the mat dozens of times. Often, it had been the much-larger Kelvin who had dropped Josh onto his back. Not once had Josh been able to get Kelvin off his feet. But Josh would keep going and keep trying.

'Then . . . begin!' the sergeant called.

Kelvin immediately leapt forward and attempted to get a hold of Josh's neck. But Josh quickly slid beneath his grasp and dashed to the other side of the mat, where he turned and faced Kelvin again.

'Good, good,' Kasula said approvingly. 'Speed and agility. Speed and agility!'

Kelvin turned and glared at Josh. 'I'll give him speed and agility!' he growled, before lunging at his opponent.

This time, Josh danced back and, with his left foot, tripped Kelvin up as he drew level with him. Kelvin fell face-first on the mat.

'Bravo, young Fulton!' said Kasula.

Josh stood looking at Kelvin in amazement. For the first time, he had put him to the mat.

Kelvin, embarrassed, looked up at Kasula. 'He got me while I was off balance!' he protested.

'Precisely!' Sergeant Kasula gave a wry smile and offered Kelvin a hand. 'Here, we have had lessons for you both. For the smaller boy – use your opponent's superior weight against him. For the larger boy – do not lose your composure or your balance. So, once more.' He waved for the pair to again take up positions facing each other.

Josh readjusted his robe. He was tired but he was pleased with himself. He had used his brains as much as he had used his muscles, and he had at last succeeded. Now, for the first time, he really believed what Sergeant Kasula had been drilling into him. He began to see the point of all this. He only hoped that Kelvin did, too.

CHAPTER 10

In the late afternoon, the heat rose up from *Canberra*'s flight deck in a dancing, distorted haze. The air temperature was almost forty degrees Celsius. As far as the eye could see, the Indian Ocean was a relatively calm Sea State 2. Yet, while *Canberra* surged along as if it were sailing up the Tanzanian coast on a flat roadway, the little patrol boat *Julius Nyere* was bucking up and down through the low swell as it strove to keep up with the big Australian warship.

Aboard *Canberra*, deck crews were scurrying around three aircraft standing on the flight deck. Two Seahawk helicopters had been brought up from the hangar deck by lift and they stood one in front of the other below the island with their rotors twirling and aircrews in place. To their left, the Heron UAV was lined up with the ski jump, its rear-facing propeller churning the air.

One of the massive deck lifts now came sliding up. Nothing more than a large square section of the deck which went up and down between the flight and hangar decks, it was bringing the members of the GRRR team to the flight deck. All members of the team were kitted out in green camouflage uniforms and had their heavy packs on their backs. They each carried their preferred weapon, from assault rifles to Baz's Minimi machinegun.

Ben was laden with a forty-kilo pack filled with his and Caesar's gear. On his belt he carried two full water canteens – one for him and one for Caesar. In one of the pouches on his belt he carried an aluminium cup that was just the right size for Caesar's tongue. On Ben's belt, too, were a sheathed Sykes commando knife, a torch, and pouches containing spare magazines for the compact Steyr automatic rifle he carried and the Browning Highpower automatic pistol holstered on his right thigh. One pouch on his belt was devoted to dog biscuits.

Signaller Brian Cisco also had his heavy-duty radio on his back, while combat medic Willy Wolf was weighed down with medical supplies as well as his own personal equipment. Every one of them was bathed in perspiration from the tropical heat. Sitting patiently at Ben's side, Caesar took in the scent of the salty sea and aviation fuel as the lift came to a shuddering halt.

The twelve-man team split in half, with the two groups striding toward the waiting Skyhawks. Charlie led one group, accompanied by Ben and Caesar, and followed by Baz, Angus Bruce, Chris Banner and Casper

Mortenson. Duke Hazard led the remaining members of the team to the second helicopter.

'Caesar, up!' Ben commanded, pointing to the heelo's interior, and the labrador immediately leapt into the cabin with an effortless bound. Once Ben had seated himself on the cabin floor with his knees up and back against the rear bulkhead, Caesar lay beside his handler, resting his chin on his paws and wrinkling his brow as he watched the others get settled. He recognised them all and felt content that the team he had come to know so well was around him. When Ben ruffled one of Caesar's ears affectionately, Caesar's tail wagged in response. Caesar knew they were off on another adventure together, and that was just how he liked it.

'Launch heelos! Launch heelos! Launch heelos!' came the voice of Lieutenant Commander Lockhart over the ship's loudspeakers.

Moments later the first Seahawk lifted into the air, angling to the left as it swung out over the ship's port side and climbed steadily away toward the unseen coast of Tanzania to the west. Once the first helicopter was clear of the ship, the second Seahawk lifted off and followed it. From a bridge window, Major Jinko watched the two choppers grow smaller in the western sky.

'Launch Heron! Launch Heron! Launch Heron!' Lockhart instructed.

The Heron's engine surged and the machine lurched forward, running across the deck. At increasing speed it slid up the ski jump, shooting into the sky as if it were a projectile released from a slingshot. Once in the air, the UAV climbed steadily as it, too, headed west. Before long, all three aircraft were lost from view.

On the bridge, Captain Rixon handed control of the ship to the XO and rose from his chair. 'Inform SOCOM that Pink Elephant's three birds are in the air,' he instructed, before heading for the door.

Major Jinko also departed the bridge. He went down to the ship's operations centre. For a few instants, he stood behind the Heron operators, looking at their trio of screens and the pictures being sent back from the UAV. Then he slipped into the seat that he would occupy for the days ahead as mission controller of Operation Pink Elephant. First looking at his watch to note the time, he tapped away at the keyboard in front of him: *0710 hours – heelos and UAV launched from* Canberra. *Operation Pink Elephant ground phase underway.*

First one blue-grey Australian Navy Seahawk and then the other descended slowly from the sky. The noise from their engines brought Leboo villagers out of their huts, but the downrush from their rotors raised such a dust cloud that the men, women and children were forced to cover their eyes and mouths and retreat. As soon as both helicopters were on the ground, their Special Forces passengers emerged, and more than one villager pointed with surprise at the brown labrador padding along beside one of the foreign soldiers.

Charlie Grover led the way to a group of Tanzanian soldiers waiting with a ranger. They stood under the shade of trees, which protected them from the fierce but dry inland heat and from the dust raised by the two choppers that remained on the ground with their engines running and rotors spinning.

A bearded man in khaki stepped forward and extended his hand to Charlie. 'Wally Springer, Chief Ranger with the Tanzanian Wildlife Service.'

'Charlie Grover,' the Australian SAS sergeant responded, shaking Springer's hand. 'I recognise you from the Tanzanian Government's video. You're Lucky's boss.'

'Nice to have another Aussie on the case, Charlie,' said Springer, leading him to a Tanzanian Army lieutenant. 'This is Lieutenant Benson Roy. He's in charge of the army detachment that's been trying to track down Lucky and the other hostages.'

Charlie took the lieutenant's hand. 'Good to meet you, sir. Sergeant Charlie Grover, Special Air Service Regiment, attached to the Global Rapid Reaction Responders.'

Roy, a young man with a lively smile, shook Charlie's hand. 'It is a pleasure to make your acquaintance, Sergeant Grover,' he said in a posh English accent.

'The lieutenant only recently returned to the army after graduating from the Royal Military Academy Sandhurst in England,' Springer informed Charlie with a slight raising of an eyebrow.

'Yes, this is my first real assignment since my return to my country,' said Roy. 'Although, I must confess, it is not proving as easy as I at first thought it would.'

'The birds have flown, Charlie,' said Springer. 'Zuba and his hostages were here yesterday, but the Tanzanian Army has lost track of them since they left.'

'They were heading west,' said Roy, 'but have disappeared.'

'My bet is that they changed course or may have doubled back,' said Springer. 'Zuba has proven a pretty tricky character. He's not your average elephant poacher. The man has a good strategic brain. Although, some people have yet to appreciate that.'

The lieutenant smiled blithely, unaware that Springer was referring to him, among others.

'How long can you keep the heelos here?' Springer asked Charlie.

Charlie checked his watch. 'Another hour or so, then they'll have to head back to the ship to refuel.'

Springer grimaced. 'Not long enough. There are thousands of square kilometres to search out there.'

'That's not the heelos' job. They will insert and extract the GRRR team, that's all. We've got a much less obvious helper up there in the heavens.' Charlie raised his eyes to the sky.

'You intend to rely on God to help you find Colonel Zuba, Sergeant?' said Lieutenant Roy, incredulous.

Charlie smiled. 'No, sir. We have a drone up there. A UAV.'

'Oh, I see,' said Roy, looking slightly embarrassed.

'I'll send the heelos back until we need them.' Charlie beckoned Brian Cisco over. When the radioman reached him, Charlie took the handset of Cisco's radio and spoke into it. 'Sally One from Oscar Zulu Leader. Receiving? Over.'

'Oscar Zulu Leader, this is Sally One,' came the reply. 'Go ahead.'

'Go home to Mama, Sally One. I'll call you when we need you.'

'Copy that, Oscar Zulu. Sally One and Sally Two going home to Mama.'

With that, the first Seahawk rose up into the air, banked left and headed toward the coast, climbing steadily as it went. The second Seahawk followed suit.

'I'll give you lot a briefing in the village schoolhouse,' Springer said as the noise of the choppers faded.

As it was a Saturday, the small building was empty. It consisted of a single room, with a ceiling of naked corrugated iron. The classroom had no desks, let alone a solid floor, and no electricity. There was no glass in the open windows. The village children crowded around outside, giggling among themselves as they watched the foreign soldiers standing on the dirt floor in front of the blackboard. None of the children was above twelve years of age – the older boys of the village, and some girls, had been taken by Colonel Zuba to become soldiers in the RAT. Some had died in battles with the Tanzanian Army, others had run away. Some were still in Zuba's ranks. These remaining youngsters were especially amused to see a big brown dog sitting with the soldiers.

'What is that dog doing there?' one bold child asked a sergeant of the Tanzanian Army.

'I think that is a war dog, child,' said the sergeant, an older man whose name was Simon Simma.

'A war dog?' said the boy, wide-eyed with surprise. 'Can it also shoot a gun, like the soldiers? It must be a very clever dog.'

'I think it is indeed a very clever dog,' said Sergeant Simma, 'but I would be very surprised if it could fire a gun. Now, all of you be quiet while Ranger Wally talks to the soldiers.'

'Will these *mzungu* soldiers catch Colonel Zuba?' asked a girl. 'He took my brothers and killed my father.'

A scowl came over Simma's face. 'I hope they catch Zuba. But now you must all be quiet.'

The children's chatter died away as Wally Springer took a laptop from his backpack and opened it on the teacher's desk at the front of the classroom. Lieutenant Roy had joined the briefing and, without saying anything, he stood to one side so that he could see what was on the laptop screen as Springer spoke to the Special Forces troops.

'This is what pays for the Revolutionary Army of Tanzania's activities,' said Springer. The chief ranger brought up an image of a dead elephant on the screen. 'This was one of hundreds of elephants killed less than a month ago, eighty kilometres from here. Poachers catch elephants with wire traps like these.' He pointed to a primitive wire contraption wrapped around the lower leg of the dead animal. 'They then come and kill the trapped elephant with rifles or spears and hack off its tusks.'

'Barbaric!' exclaimed Angus Bruce. 'Absolutely barbaric!'

'It turned out that my rangers and I were only about half an hour away from where the poachers were operating. They used a shotgun to speed up the removal of the tusks.'

Caesar was shifting restlessly at Ben's feet, and Ben reached forward and patted him reassuringly. He knew that Caesar was picking up a variety of new scents from the earthen floor. To Caesar, every living thing had a distinctive scent. Children in the inland parts of Tanzania had a very different diet to that of Josh and Maddie and the other children that Caesar was accustomed to in Australia. They ate a lot of bananas and very little meat, so their scents, to Caesar, were very different, and took a little getting used to.

'Where do the elephant tusks go, once the poachers have them?' Ben asked Wally.

'They send the tusks in shipping containers to sea ports and ship them to China, Japan and elsewhere in East Asia.'

'Why to China and Japan, may I ask?' said Jean-Claude.

'Elephant tusks are pure ivory – a fine-grained form of dentine,' Springer replied. 'It is highly prized in Asia, and in China in particular. They use it for all the sorts of things that you see in every tourist shop in Hong Kong.' He brought up a picture of ivory statues, ivory chopsticks and intricate ivory jewellery. 'The Chinese also grind ivory down to use in certain medicines and folk remedies.'

'And elephants die just for that?' said Casper. 'The hunters don't even eat the elephant meat?'

Springer shook his head. 'Even when local farmers sometimes kill elephants to protect their crops from

114

being trampled, they never eat the elephant's flesh. For one thing, it's too tough.'

'Such a waste of a noble animal,' said Willy Wolf, shaking his head.

'The elephant only has one enemy in the wild,' said Springer, 'and that's us human beings. Elephants have nothing to fear from any other animal. We humans are its only enemy, all because some people like shiny ivory souvenirs.' He said this with disgust.

'Why doesn't the Chinese Government stop the importation of ivory?' said Chris Banner.

Springer smiled a wry smile. 'Officially, the Chinese Government says that it only permits the legal importation of sixty-seven tonnes of ivory each year, and that it cracks down on illegal imports. But that sixty-seven tonnes represents thousands of butchered elephants. Even so, the Chinese turn a blind eye to much of the smuggling of additional ivory into their country. Ivory carving and selling is a multi-billion-dollar industry in China, with tens of thousands of people employed by it.'

'Is the importation of ivory illegal in the US?' asked Tim McHenry.

'It is,' Springer replied, 'but at the same time it's not illegal to sell ivory products in the US, so that in itself encourages the illegal ivory imports. US ivory imports, though, pale in comparison to those going from Africa to Asia. Some Asian countries like the Philippines and Thailand are cracking down on the sale of ivory products, but ivory is freely and massively available in China. Demand in China for elephant tusks has actually *increased*, sending the price way up – it's gone from one hundred and fifty dollars per kilogram six years ago to one thousand dollars per kilogram today.'

This generated low whistles from around the room.

'Ivory now rates alongside illegal drugs as a money-maker for criminals,' Springer added, 'and it is Zuba's sole source of income, for his army and himself. The villagers here in Leboo tell us that Zuba is hard-up for cash right now, so he's obviously still waiting to be paid for his last ivory haul. And he'll keep on making money from killing elephants unless he's stopped.'

'The Tanzanian Government seems serious about stopping the poaching,' said Baz. 'That's why they hired Lucky, wasn't it?'

Springer nodded. 'They are serious. But until all the poachers are caught, there will always be a trade in illegal ivory. And as you know, the poachers are better armed than most of the government's men.'

'Can't the authorities stop the ivory getting out of the country?' Angus Bruce asked. 'They have to choke off the supply.'

'Easier said than done,' Springer replied with a sigh. 'We know that there are Chinese and Japanese merchants living here, in Tanzania, who arrange the export of the poached tusks for a handsome cut of the profits. But the local police have never been able to catch them in the act. There is so much money involved, and we suspect that some police are taking bribes from the merchants to look the other way.'

'Why not approach the problem from the other end?' Jean-Claude suggested. 'Cut off demand for ivory. If no one could sell ivory in China, there would be no market for it. The Chinese Government must ban the sale of ivory.'

Willy Wolf agreed. 'If there was no market for ivory, there would be no need to kill elephants. The poaching would stop.'

'Exactly,' said Lyon. 'Is this not a simple solution to the problem?'

Springer shook his head. 'There would have to be massive and sustained international pressure on the Chinese Government for that to happen. Unfortunately, most governments around the world are more interested in things other than saving the elephant.'

'Elephants don't get to vote,' Duke Hazard said cynically, 'so politicians ignore them.'

'Then perhaps ordinary folk around the world should be putting a wee bit of pressure on the Chinese Government to ban the sale of ivory products,' said Sergeant Bruce. 'An international petition signed by millions of ordinary people to save the elephants.'

'Who's going to get that petition up, Bruce?' Hazard queried, sounding sceptical.

'Someone should,' Angus replied.

Hazard chuckled. 'Like who? You? Good luck with that, buddy.'

Conversation erupted among the GRRR members around the classroom.

'Hang on,' called Ben. 'Our chief concern right now is saving Lucky and the other hostages.'

'You got that right, Ben,' Tim McHenry agreed.

'Too right!' Baz echoed. 'And Major Jinko said the shrinks reckoned that Zuba could lose his cool and turn on Lucky and the other hostages within forty-eight hours.'

'I doubt that,' said Chief Ranger Springer. 'Zuba has been a thorn in my side for two years now. I've got to know how he operates. He doesn't lose his cool or kill on a whim. Yes, Zuba has a big ego, but he is a clever, calculating operator and he likes the power that he thinks holding hostages gives him. Lucky is his ace card. I think Zuba's prepared to hang onto Lucky for months, or even years!'

'We could be here for a while, then, people,' said Duke Hazard, stuffing a piece of gum into his mouth and commencing to chew vigorously.

Half-a-dozen new conversations began in the room as views were put forward on everything from Zuba's character to the best way to end the ivory trade.

Charlie had been taking in the conversation. Only now did he put up a hand and raise his voice to be heard above all the talk in the room. 'Let's focus on the mission at hand, you blokes!' The room fell silent as Charlie turned to face the other members of the team. 'The big problem is, we don't know where Zuba and the hostages are. Until we do, we can't do a thing.'

'No, not a thing, man!' Chris Banner concurred.

'What if we made Zuba come to us, Charlie?' said Ben, and all eyes turned to him.

'How do we do that, mate?' Charlie asked.

'What if one of us posed as an ivory merchant who was prepared to pay Zuba fifteen hundred dollars a kilogram for his next batch of tusks? We could lure him to a meet and capture him! From all we've learned about Zuba, I think his so-called army would fall apart once we had Zuba in custody. His "soldiers" are only kids. After that, the release of Lucky and the other hostages should be easy to accomplish.'

A smile creased Charlie's face. 'Not a bad plan, Ben. Not a bad plan at all. Who did you have in mind for the job of ivory merchant?'

Ben turned his eyes to the one member of the team who had not spoken a word the entire time they'd been in the classroom. 'Toushi,' he said.

'Aha!' Charlie exclaimed, as everyone looked at Toushi Harada. 'Good thinking, mate.'

'But I am a computer expert, not an expert in ivory,' Toushi protested.

'Zuba wouldn't know that until he met you,' said Charlie, his mind racing with ways and means to make Ben's idea work. 'And by that time he'd be in our net.'

'What makes you think that Zuba would come to a meeting with a new ivory merchant, and so soon?' Wally said sceptically.

'Would the tusks from that recent kill you showed us have left the country yet?' Ben asked.

'I doubt it. I estimate it'd take about a month for those tusks to get to the port. They're probably sitting in a shipping container on the dock at Dar es Salaam as we speak, labelled as agricultural produce and waiting to be shipped off to Asia.'

'You're sure it would be going out of Dar es Salaam?' Charlie queried.

Springer nodded. 'Ninety-five per cent of Tanzania's exports leave from Dar es Salaam.'

'Wouldn't the ivory smugglers use a small out-of-the-way port to evade attention?' Angus Bruce asked.

'No. The larger and busier the port, the easier it is to blend into the background,' said Springer. 'Besides, half the port of Dar es Salaam is controlled by TICTS, a Chinese-owned syndicate based in Hong Kong. The Tanzanian Government allows TICTS to check and clear its own cargo without any involvement from

Tanzania's customs inspectors. I wouldn't be surprised if those companies, or some of their Chinese employees, are involved in the illegal export of ivory. You can bet your last dollar the ivory smugglers will have this latest ivory haul there, hidden among genuine exports, waiting for a ship from China to take it away.'

'Could we organise a search of the dock?' asked Ben.

'The Tanzanian Customs Service doesn't have the manpower to conduct one,' Springer replied.

Ben smiled. 'But *we* have the manpower. Or, should I say, we have the dog power.' He reached forward and gave Caesar a pat.

Caesar turned his head toward him and began wagging his tail on the dusty floor. The look on his face seemed to say, *Are you talking about me, boss?*

Springer frowned. 'I don't quite understand, Sergeant. Is your dog trained to find ivory? Because if it isn't –'

'No, Caesar isn't trained to locate ivory,' Ben replied, 'but he can track down minute amounts of explosives residue.'

'How does that help?'

'You said the poachers used a shotgun to help remove the tusks this last time?'

'Yes,' replied Springer, still unconvinced.

'Then there will be gunshot residue on the end of each of those tusks,' said Ben. 'Enough for Caesar to sniff it out.'

Springer's mouth dropped open in astonishment. 'You're joking?'

'No, he's not joking,' said Charlie. 'Caesar is a super-sniffer.' He turned to Ben, a grin widening on his face. 'Good thinking, mate. If we can locate and seize that latest ivory shipment and make a big noise about it so that Zuba hears of it, he'll be desperate for cash. And we might just be able to lure him into a meet with Toushi.'

'Especially if Toushi offers to give him money up-front at the meeting,' Ben suggested.

Charlie nodded. 'Roger to that. But one step at a time. First, we have to locate the ivory at the port.'

'We have to get Ben and Caesar to Dar es Salaam, fast,' said Baz urgently. 'Ask Mama to send one of the Sallys to give them a ride.'

'Hold your horses,' said Duke Hazard. 'You better check with Papa first, Grover. He might not like the idea of branching out into the customs business.'

'Right on it.' Charlie beckoned Brian Cisco to follow him outside to radio Major Jinko aboard *Canberra*. Before long, Charlie had spoken with the major and the pair returned. 'Papa has authorised us to proceed with the Dar es Salaam mission,' he informed the team. 'SOCOM will alert the Tanzanian authorities to what we're doing and get their cooperation. Ben, Papa says that Baz and Chris Banner are to go with you and Caesar as backup. A heelo is on its way from Mama to fly the four of you down to the port. Take only essential gear.'

'Roger that,' Ben acknowledged, beginning to strip his heavy pack from his back.

'You'd better take one of Lieutenant Roy's men with you,' Springer suggested, 'to help deal with the local authorities down there.'

'A very good idea,' said Lieutenant Roy. 'I will detach Sergeant Simma to accompany the men with the dog.'

'Thanks, Lieutenant.' Charlie turned back to Ben. 'Papa has given you a maximum of six hours on the ground to find the ivory shipment. Do you reckon you can do it in that timeframe?'

'Caesar won't let us down,' Ben assured the team, easing his pack to the floor.

Caesar, sensing imminent activity, came to his feet with his tail wagging. He looked up at Ben expectantly, as if to say, *Are we going to play now, boss? Ready when you are!*

CHAPTER 11

Josh Fulton looked down at Kelvin Corbett lying at his feet.

'It's not fair!' Kelvin whined. He glared in the direction of Iron Fist Kasula, who stood watching them from the edge of the mat. 'You taught Josh how to put me on the floor every time.'

Kasula nodded. 'It's true.'

'I can't win!' Almost in tears, Kelvin slowly sat up.

'But I have taught *both* of you exactly the same techniques, Kelvin,' the sergeant responded. 'You thought that, being the bigger boy, you would always defeat smaller boys like Josh. But, now, you see that's not the case.'

Josh offered Kelvin his hand, but the larger boy peevishly knocked it away and came to his feet under his own steam. 'You've been favouring Josh because his dad's a soldier like you!' he declared, before stalking off to the change rooms.

'Come back,' Kasula ordered. 'We are not finished yet.'

'*I* am!' Kelvin called back over his shoulder. 'I've had enough of all this garbage! I quit!'

'You can't quit, Kelvin!' Josh protested. 'We both agreed to do this course. So did our parents.'

'I don't care!' Kelvin shot back as he kept on walking.

In the darkness, two guards led Lucky to a camp site. They arrived to find RAT soldiers and the new recruits sitting cross-legged around a cooking fire, eating with their fingers from several large shared bowls. Colonel Zuba sat in their midst, raised above them all by a small folding stool. Even though it was night-time, Zuba still wore his sunglasses. He watched on as Captain Chawinga leaned over a large saucepan on the fire and stirred it with a wooden ladle.

When Zuba saw Lucky, he broke into a smile. 'So, Ranger Lucky,' he said, 'come, sit beside me.' He pointed to his left side, and two soldiers sitting there quickly moved to make a place for the newcomer.

The guards pressed the ranger down to sit beside their leader. Lucky cast his gaze around the new recruits, taking in the boys' haggard faces and fearful eyes in the firelight. 'Look at these kids,' he said. 'They're just as much your prisoners as I am, Zuba. Why don't you let them go? A good friend of mine has a son, back in

Australia, around the same age as these boys, and he is much too young to be a soldier. Let them be children for a few more years. Only men should have to fight wars.'

'I will *make* men of them!' Zuba said fiercely. 'For the moment, it is true that these little ones are missing their mummies. They will get over it. They have a fine meal of goat meat. Not since the last wedding in their village would these boys have eaten meat. In *my* army, they will eat much meat and grow strong, and these boys will live to thank me for it.'

'Stolen meat,' Lucky corrected.

Zuba shrugged. 'A man's stomach does not care where meat comes from, only where it goes.'

'Stealing the livestock of the people you claim to be fighting for is not a good way to win their loyalty, I would have thought.'

Zuba shook his head in disagreement. 'The people of Leboo should be pleased to donate a goat or two to our patriotic cause. But enough of goats. Drink chai with us.' He nodded to his deputy, who was pouring the contents of the saucepan into a large metal teapot. 'Chawinga, a mug also for our guest.'

'Yes, Colonel,' Chawinga replied. He filled several mugs with the steaming contents of the teapot. First, he handed one mug to Zuba, then he held out another to Lucky. 'Drink,' he said. 'It is chai – water, milk, black tea, cardamom, ginger and sugar.'

Lucky accepted the mug but waited until he saw Zuba drink from his.

Seeing this, Chawinga chuckled. 'This is not poisoned, Ranger Lucky. Drink. This is good. This is the national drink of Tanzania.'

Smiling, Zuba took a sip from his mug. 'As Chawinga says, it is neither drugged nor poisoned. Enjoy.'

Now Lucky tasted Chawinga's brew, and he had to agree that the chai was delicious. Taking another sip, he watched Chawinga wander over to sit on the periphery of the group. Chawinga was clearly a solitary sort of man, with no friends among the soldiers he helped to command.

'So, now we will talk of important matters,' said Zuba, regaining Lucky's attention.

'What sort of important matters?' Lucky asked warily.

'What nationality are you, Ranger Lucky? You sound to me like Chief Ranger Springer – an Australian.'

'I was born in New Zealand,' Lucky answered, 'but when I joined the Australian Army I took dual Australian–New Zealand citizenship.'

This pleased the rebel leader. 'Good, very good. That is two governments that will pay to have you returned.'

'Is that all you think about?' Lucky boldly asked. 'Money?'

'The leader of a revolutionary army must think about money,' Zuba replied. 'Without money, how would I pay and equip my soldiers?'

This surprised Lucky. 'You pay these boys?'

'Of course. I pay them five dollars a month. If they stay with me for many years they will all be rich men, able to buy their own farms.'

'Not at five dollars a month, they won't,' Lucky scoffed.

Zuba chose to ignore this comment. 'The Tanzanian Government would not pay such money for you. They would not pay one dollar for the return of their own people. But for you, the governments of Australia and New Zealand will, I think, pay a lot of money. And for this, I want you to write them a letter.' Reaching inside his jacket, Zuba produced a notepad and ballpoint pen, which he thrust at Lucky. 'You will write what I tell you,' he instructed.

Lucky ignored the pad and pen. 'Don't waste your time, Zuba. The governments of Australia and New Zealand don't bargain with terrorists.'

Zuba's face dropped. 'I am not a terrorist! I am a freedom fighter!'

'Not in the eyes of the world. Prove that you're not a terrorist – let me go. Let my rangers go. Let these boys go. Lay down your arms.'

Zuba smiled slyly. 'I am not a terrorist and I am not a fool. Do you know what I think, Ranger Lucky? I think you expect the authorities to rescue you. Well, let me tell you, they have not been able to find me for two years and they will not find me now. And it will not be any use sending more *mzungu* such as yourself to try to find you. Foreigners cannot know this part of the world the way my soldiers and I do.'

'Well, for one thing, you don't have the technology that governments do,' Lucky countered.

'Technology?' Chuckling to himself, Zuba reached into a pocket of his tunic, withdrawing a rectangular object and holding it up for Lucky to see. 'Here is *my* technology, my friend. The only technology that I need out here in the bush.'

Lucky frowned as he tried to make out the object in the dark. 'What's that?'

'This is a transistor radio that I have had for many years. Every night I listen to the Tanzanian Government radio service and to the BBC World Service from London. You may have thought to yourself that Abraham Zuba speaks very good English for a man who never went to school. Well, as a boy, I taught myself English, listening to the BBC World Service on this very transistor radio.' Zuba smiled wide. 'Do you not find me to be articulate?'

'Yes, very articulate,' Lucky conceded.

'And do you know what my little transistor radio is telling me now, Ranger Lucky? It is silent about you. Neither the BBC World Service nor the Tanzanian Government radio any longer speak of your capture by myself, or the fact that you are missing. Another rebel army leader would be unhappy that he was no longer a subject of news broadcasts, but not Abraham Zuba. You see, this tells me that the government is no longer interested in finding you, Ranger Lucky. They have given up on you!' He raised his eyebrows. 'So, no one will be trying to rescue you, my friend. The Tanzanian Government has stopped looking for you. Now we must tell the governments of Australia and New Zealand that you are alive, well and available – at a handsome price. Here, take these and write what I tell you.' His smile evaporated. 'Or I will shoot one of your rangers!'

Unhappily, Lucky reached up with his bound hands and took the notepad. 'I can't write with my hands tied,' he protested. 'Untie me.'

'No, I think not. We cannot have you attempting to escape our custody, my friend. Write as best you can with your hands tied.'

Lucky glared back at him defiantly.

'Do you want me to shoot one of your rangers?' Zuba said impatiently. 'I will shoot them all, starting with the youngest, if you do not do as I say! Put from your mind all thoughts of being rescued. You will be my prisoner for a long, long time if you do not write this letter.'

With a sigh, Lucky rested the notepad on his lap, then took the pen from Zuba. 'Okay, go ahead. What do you want me to say?'

From the open doorway of the low-flying Seahawk, Ben looked out over the sprawling city of Dar es Salaam, and beyond it, the blue-green Indian Ocean. From the small amount of research on Tanzania that he had been able to do prior to this operation, he knew that the city had a population of more than four million people, many of whom lived in slums. The city's port district of Temeke was easy to find. A bluff point lined with docks poked out into a natural harbour, and a score of large cargo ships were either tied up at the docks or at anchor in the bay.

As the Royal Australian Navy helicopter carrying Ben, Caesar and their three companions flew closer to the port, the pilot's voice crackled in the headset covering Ben's ears.

'Sergeant Fulton,' he said, 'I've just been talking with the Port Authority. They say there's no place for us to land at the port. I think they'd prefer it if we just went away.'

Ben smiled faintly. 'Not a problem. We'll rappel down.'

'Roger that,' said the pilot. 'Prepare for rappelling.'

To the astonishment of the hundreds of men working on the docks, the chopper arrived at the port's front gate and loudly hovered above it. Men driving forklifts almost ran off the road in their surprise and curiosity at the unusual sight. Rappelling lines dropped down from both sides of the Seahawk, followed by three soldiers rapidly sliding to the ground. To further amaze the watching men, a large brown dog was lowered down, followed by a terrified Sergeant Simon Simma. The sergeant had never even been in a helicopter before in his life, let alone been lowered from one. Simma went very pale, and the military cap on his head was knocked flying as he descended, but he made it in one piece and gratefully removed the lowering sling from under his arms once his feet were on solid ground.

With its passengers off-loaded, the heelo lifted away, reeling in the rappelling lines as it climbed and headed back out to sea to once again reunite with *Canberra*. Sally One would return in six hours' time. With the Seahawk disappearing to the east, Ben looked around as Baz, Chris and Sergeant Simma joined him. Already, the steamy coastal heat was coating his brow with perspiration. Dar es Salaam was close to the equator, and was one of the hottest, most humid cities in the world.

A scowling port official – a tall, gaunt man with thick glasses, wearing shorts and a short-sleeved shirt complete with a necktie – came striding toward them from an office at the gate. 'What do you think you are doing?' he demanded.

Ben, who had been clipping Caesar's metal leash in place, came to his feet. 'We're the Global Rapid Reaction Responders, sir. A specialist unit of the United Nations.'

'Never heard of it.' The official was clearly not in a cooperative mood.

'Well, whether you've heard of it or not, sir,' Ben replied, 'we are conducting a search for contraband in the TICTS area of the port.'

'On whose authority?'

'On the authority of Minister Benjamin Kadanka.' This was the Tanzanian cabinet minister who had asked the UN for help with rescuing Lucky Mertz and catching Abraham Zuba.

'Benjamin Kadanka is Minister for Natural Resources and Tourism,' the official scoffed. 'He has no authority here at the port.'

'I think you'll find he does, sir,' said Ben.

Sergeant Simma produced a letter from his pocket, unfolded it and held it up for the man to read. It was signed by the country's Minister for Police, granting permission for the members of GRRR to go wherever they liked if they had a reasonable suspicion that they would discover evidence of a crime.

'We're looking for contraband ivory, Tanzania's most precious natural resource,' said Ben, leading Caesar past the official and around the port entrance's boom gate.

Baz and Chris followed close behind them, leaving the official standing there, blustering uselessly. Sergeant Simma was the last to pass the official. As he did, he poked his tongue out at him.

In the TICTS half of the port, thousands of metal shipping containers the size of large trucks sat side by side, stacked one atop the other, across the bitumen dockside loading area. The small GRRR detachment working here was dwarfed by the stacks and by massive, four-wheeled lifting machines that looked like praying mantises. The sun had gone down, and now the docks were lit by banks of orange lights.

With the sunset had come the evening cool. Both Ben and Caesar were grateful for that. They had been searching for six hours without success. Ben had given his four-legged partner a break every hour and a drink of water from one of the two water canteens on his belt. The canteens had been filled on *Canberra*, which produced its own fresh water by evaporating seawater in a large desalination plant aboard. This was the only water that Ben would permit Caesar to drink here at the port. He didn't trust the quality of the local water, which might contain any number of diseases.

As night wrapped around them, they worked on in the artificial light. There was no way that Ben and

Caesar could have searched every single container in six hours. They might have accomplished it in six days. So, Ben had been selective, picking containers for inspection at random, taking special interest in those whose paperwork indicated they were carrying agricultural produce – which Wally Springer had said was the usual cover for smuggled ivory.

To complicate matters, the seal on each container had to be broken and the doors unlocked for Caesar to check their contents. In order to do this, the assistance of a TICTS official was needed. Baz and Chris had gone in search of just such a man and had found an English-speaking Chinese clerk by the name of Mr Zhu working on the second floor of a TICTS office in a dockside warehouse. The middle-aged Mr Zhu had been reluctant to cooperate, but Baz and Chris hadn't let that get in their way.

'This isn't a request and it isn't an invitation,' Baz had told Mr Zhu. 'You are going to help us look inside the containers, end of story! A mate of mine is in trouble, and you are going to help us get him out of trouble.'

Mr Zhu was brought down to the piers. He opened one container after another, looking very nervous as Ben let Caesar poke his nose inside each one. But as time ticked by, Caesar found nothing.

'You're pushing him pretty hard, Ben,' Chris Banner said with concern, when Caesar took a drink break.

'I know,' Ben said grimly. 'He's pretty much at the limit of his endurance now. Some dogs lose interest in the job after a while, but Caesar would sniff until he dropped.' Kneeling beside his partner, Ben ruffled Caesar's neck. 'Wouldn't you, mate?'

In response, Caesar wearily licked him on the cheek.

From the seaward side of the port came the buzzing sound of an approaching helicopter.

'That's the Sally coming to pick us up, Ben,' said Baz. 'I think we're done here. Don't you, mate?'

'I don't like giving up,' Ben replied with a sigh.

'Hey, man, we could always announce that we found the ivory shipment,' Chris suggested with a grin. 'How would Zuba know the difference?'

'His mates at the port would tell him that we hadn't found it,' Ben replied.

'But who's he going to believe?'

'I'd rather find the real ivory haul.' Ben leaned close to his EDD. 'What do you reckon, Caesar? We check one last container before we call it quits?' Caesar's tail began to wag. 'Okay, Caesar's up for it,' he declared with a smile, giving the labrador another pat before coming to his feet.

Taking hold of Caesar's leash, Ben walked to the next row of shipping containers and stopped to look up at a blue container sitting on top of another.

'That one?' asked Baz, lugging an aluminium ladder that he and Chris had found in a wharf shed.

Ben nodded. 'Yep, that one will do.'

Baz placed one end of the ladder against the bottom of the upper container, then turned to Mr Zhu. 'Up you go, sunshine. Open her up, there's a good man.'

Mr Zhu shook his head. 'It a waste of time. I no do.'

'It's not your decision to make, my friend,' said Chris, taking Mr Zhu by the shoulders and marching him to the foot of the ladder. He pointed upwards. 'Climb!'

'Like I say, all waste of time,' Mr Zhu protested. Slowly, he climbed the ladder. He removed the seal and opened the doors. Then back down the ladder he came.

'Okay, mate,' said Ben. 'One last time.' He unclipped Caesar's leash and pointed up the ladder. 'Caesar, seek on!'

Tail wagging, Caesar launched himself onto the rungs of the ladder. He climbed nimbly to the top, and as he poked his nose into the open container, he became very restless. Caesar looked at Ben, then into the container again, then at the rungs of the ladder.

'Something's up,' Ben announced. 'Come back down, Caesar. Back down here, mate.' He pointed to the bitumen beside him and let out the recall whistle.

Caesar obeyed instantly. But he was much more slow and uncertain coming back down the ladder than he had been going up. Once he had four legs on the ground, he did an odd circle on the spot, looked back up at the container, then sat down, with his gaze fixed firmly on the container's opening.

'Bingo!' exclaimed Baz. 'That's Caesar's signature, isn't it? Caesar has found something.'

'Looks like it to me. Caesar, stay.' Ben set off up the ladder. Once he looked in through the open doors, he was confronted with a wall of hessian sacks stamped 'GROUND CARDAMOM, Product of Tanzania'. Taking hold of the corner of one sack, he dragged it out and threw it to the ground below.

'No do that! No do that!' Mr Zhu protested, waving his arms about. 'Damage goods!'

Ben ignored him, pulling out and dumping another half-a-dozen sacks, to Mr Zhu's dismay. Then he took a torch from a clip on his belt and shone it into the container's interior, through the gap in the wall of cardamom sacks that he had created. In the torch beam, he saw more sacks, with long curved shapes inside.

'That's it!' he exclaimed, poking his head out of the container. 'We've found Zuba's ivory shipment!' Ben, his elation overcoming his weariness now that they had found what they were looking for after six hours of searching, scrambled down the ladder. 'Chris, you can do the honours.'

Chris climbed into the container and removed every sack of elephant tusks for confiscation and burning.

It would turn out that eighty per cent of the contents of the container were illegal ivory.

Caesar had been sitting patiently watching his master up on the ladder. Now that Ben was back on the ground, Caesar's tail began to wag. But the labrador was too well trained to move. Ben dropped to one knee beside him and, pulling his head in close and patting him vigorously, exclaimed, 'You've done it again, Caesar! Well done, mate! Well done!'

'Super-sniffer strikes again,' Baz said with a laugh, turning to Mr Zhu. 'Mate, someone has a lot of explaining to do. Let's start with you.' Chris tossed down another sack filled with elephant trunks. It landed with a dull thud at Baz's feet. Pointing to the sack, Baz demanded, 'Where did this illegal ivory shipment come from?'

Mr Zhu paled. 'Nothing to do with me!' he protested. 'I know nothing about this.'

Baz raised his eyebrows. 'Mr Zhu, mate, that's what they all say.'

That same Saturday, Nan and Maddie Fulton were walking hand in hand along a busy shopping street in Holsworthy.

'But I still don't know what ivory is, Nan,' said Maddie, as Nan paused to look in the window of a dress shop. 'How can it be an elephant's tusk one minute, and then ivory once it's been chopped off the poor elephant? Why don't they just call it "elephant's tusk" all the time?'

Nan smiled to herself. 'The word "ivory" sounds much nicer, Maddie. I don't think many people would be as interested in buying it if someone said "Buy this statue made from elephant tusk and put it on a shelf to show it off" or "Buy this jewellery made from elephant tusk and hang it around your neck".'

'So, is an elephant's tusk like our bones?'

'Yes, sort of.'

'Then, why do people buy elephant bones and put them on their shelves?'

'Because ivory is shiny and rare, and it can be carved into really intricate shapes.'

Maddie frowned. 'But elephants need their tusks. Otherwise, they wouldn't be born with them, would they? That's like selling people's arms because our arm bones could be carved into inticklate shapes. Isn't it?'

'In a way, yes,' Nan conceded. She looked down at her granddaughter. 'You know what, Maddie? I don't think a lot of people know that ivory is actually the tusks of elephants.'

'That dericulous!' Maddie exclaimed, screwing up her face and folding her arms. 'People should know that!'

'Well, when you look at ivory, it doesn't look like an elephant's tusk.'

'What does it look like, then?'

For a moment, Nan was stumped for an answer, and then she remembered something. 'Last week, there was a display in the jeweller's window in the next street. I'm sure there was an antique ivory necklace among it. Come on, we'll see if it's still there.'

Taking hold of Maddie's hand, Nan led her along the pavement and around the corner to an old-fashioned shopfront.

'Look, it's still there,' said Nan, pointing to a red felt display board in the shop window that was labelled 'Rare Antique Estate Jewellery'. Attached to the board were old necklaces, rings, earrings and even a tiara. Most featured silver settings and sparkled with diamonds, emeralds and rubies. But one necklace was yellow in colour and featured dozens of finely carved pieces strung together. 'That's an antique ivory necklace!' Nan declared, pointing to it. 'It's probably one hundred and fifty years old and worth a small fortune.'

'That's ivory?' Maddie said with surprise. 'It doesn't look like an elephant's tusk.'

'But it is. An elephant had to die for that ivory to fall into the hands of the man who carved that necklace.'

'Why isn't there a sign that says it's made from dead elephant?' Maddie wanted to know.

'I suppose, Maddie dear, the shop people don't think that's important.'

'Well, I do!' Maddie declared. Letting go of Nan's hand, she marched in through the shop's doorway.

'Maddie!' Nan called, setting off after her. 'Where are you going?'

Inside the jeweller's store, there were three salespeople behind the glass counter, two of whom were talking with customers. Maddie marched up to the third salesperson, the manager, a smartly dressed woman in her fifties.

The woman looked down at Maddie on the other side of the counter, and smiled. 'Hello there. What can I do for you, sweetie?'

'You've got dead elephant in your window!' Maddie announced. 'And it's hobble!'

The smile froze on the manager's face. 'I beg your pardon?'

Maddie's eyes narrowed and she folded her arms. 'In the window. The necklace. It's made from an elephant's tusk. That's hobble!'

The manager's smile quickly became a frown. 'Excuse me?'

By this time, Nan had caught up with Maddie. 'My granddaughter doesn't approve of your ivory necklace in the window,' she explained, placing her hands protectively on Maddie's shoulders.

'Oh.' The manager smiled. 'It's an antique necklace, dear,' she said to Maddie, patronisingly. 'Very old.'

'Doesn't matter,' Maddie retorted. 'Someone killed an elephant to make it. It shouldn't be allowed.'

Nan steered Maddie toward the door. 'Someone has to take a stand against ivory poaching,' she said over her shoulder.

The manager's face clouded over. 'Not in my shop, they won't!' she huffed, ignoring the other customers who had turned to look at her. 'Anyway, it's too late for *that* elephant!'

Outside, Nan and Maddie resumed walking side by side.

'You're not mad at me, are you, Nan?' asked Maddie. 'For telling the lady about the dead elephant tusk in her window?'

Nan smiled. 'No, Maddie dear, I'm not mad at you. In fact, I'm rather proud of you for speaking out.'

Maddie beamed. 'Good!'

'Yes, very proud,' said Nan.

'Who else can we tell to stop killing elephants?'

'I think that's enough for today.'

'Joshie!' Maddie suddenly exclaimed.

A familiar face appeared in the crowd ahead. Josh and his best friend Baxter Chung waved and walked up to the pair.

'Josh, what are you doing here?' asked Nan. 'Why aren't you with Sergeant Kasula?'

Josh shrugged. 'Kelvin quit the course.'

'What? When?'

'During the week. Just because he wasn't winning anymore.' A triumphant smile came over Josh's face. 'After he put me on the mat for weeks, I learned how to put him on the mat, Nan. Even though he's a lot bigger than me.'

'Why didn't you tell me this earlier?'

Avoiding Nan's gaze, Josh didn't reply.

'So, Kelvin just gave up?'

Josh nodded. 'He said it wasn't fair that I was beating him.'

'That's not how it works, I'm afraid,' said Nan. 'Kelvin can't just give up because he's not winning. That's the easy way out. His mother and I agreed that he would see that course through with you. And see it through he will. Come on.' Turning in the opposite direction, she led Maddie away. 'You too, Josh.'

Josh glanced at Baxter unhappily. 'Nan, where are you going?'

'We're going to pay the Corbetts a visit. I bet Kelvin's mother doesn't know he chickened out of the course.'

'Oh, Nan!' Josh protested. He hated it when Nan took on the Corbetts.

Nan looked back over her shoulder. 'Come along, Josh. My car's just around the corner. Say goodbye to Baxter.'

Begrudgingly, Josh farewelled Baxter then trailed after Nan and Maddie. 'Can I please just stay in the car when you talk to Mrs Corbett?' he asked, when they reached the car.

'No, you cannot stay in the car. This is all about you and Kelvin, Josh, in case you'd forgotten. He bullied you, remember? And you hid it from us. This was part of his rehabilitation. Neither he nor you can get out of it.' Opening a door to the car, Nan pointed to the back seat. 'In you get, young man.'

'It's so embarrassing when grown-ups argue about us kids in front of us,' Josh said, clambering into the back. Maddie quickly slid in after him.

'There will be no arguing,' Nan assured him. 'Mrs Corbett and I are in complete agreement on this. Kelvin has no easy options here. Nor do you, young man.'

'It wasn't my idea for Kelvin to quit,' Josh protested. 'But now he has, there's no need for me to go back to Iron Fist on my own.'

'Your father thinks the training with Sergeant Kasula will do you both good, and so do I. Seatbelts done up please, the pair of you!' Nan instructed as she put the key in the ignition. 'That includes you, young man!'

Josh pulled a face. 'I'm always "young man" when you're cross with me,' he said under his breath. 'I didn't do anything wrong.'

Nan Fulton eyed him in the rear-view mirror. 'You didn't tell me until today that Kelvin had quit the course. Now, do as I say and do up your seatbelt.'

'Yes, Nan,' sighed Josh. He'd planned to slump down in the seat so that none of his schoolmates saw him in his grandmother's car on the way to Kelvin's place. Now, as he clicked the seatbelt in place, he felt like a prisoner on display for the whole world to see.

'Ranger Lucky, can you ask Colonel Zuba's men to untie our hands?' Koinet pleaded. All six of the captive rangers sat crammed together in the back of the bumping Land Rover. 'It is so uncomfortable. You speak with Colonel Zuba all the time. Tell him that I will not try to run away if he unties me.'

'Hush, child,' old Julius said wearily. 'Bear this like a man, as Ranger Lucky bears it, as we all bear it.'

'I am not a man,' Koinet replied sourly. 'I am only a boy.'

'And boys have to grow up pretty quickly,' Lucky remarked, 'especially in this part of the world.'

Koinet lapsed into a morose silence as the Land Rover drove on.

In the early hours of the morning, Zuba's convoy came to a halt. The canvas cover on the back of the Land Rover was thrown back.

'Out!' commanded one of the guards gruffly, and Lucky and his fellow rangers stiffly clambered out.

The vehicles had stopped beside an expanse of water that, in the light of the rising moon, stretched to the horizon. Lucky had made it his business to lodge a map of Tanzania firmly in his mind when he'd started work in this country, and he knew that this must be Lake Victoria. There was a small village here, lit by oil torches that stretched along the edge of a narrow beach. A single, spindly jetty jutted out into the flat water. Tied to it was an old blue ex-military landing craft with faded Tanzanian Army markings. A number of small wooden boats were also moored to the jetty and drawn up on the beach either side of it.

Men from the village came to meet Zuba and his rebel band, and Lucky watched as they shook hands with Zuba and Chawinga and embraced them. There were smiles all around, but as the conversation continued, Lucky could see that the village men had quickly become unhappy. An argument broke out between Zuba and one of the headmen from the village.

'What are they arguing about, Julius?' Lucky asked. He and his rangers stood on the sand with their guards, watching them closely.

'I don't know,' Julius replied. 'We are too far away for me to hear clearly.'

'I wouldn't be surprised if it was about money,' Lucky said half to himself. 'The locals were expecting a payout for their help, but Zuba has run out of money.'

Julius nodded. 'That sounds right to me.'

As they continued to watch, they saw Zuba angrily turn to one of his men. Taking the soldier's AK-47 from the man's hands, Zuba directed it toward the nearest livestock compound and fired. The burst of gunfire chopped down a section of fence, sprayed red earth into the air and felled several of the cows penned inside the compound. Zuba's older soldiers thought this was hilarious and roared with laughter.

In this part of the world, a man's wealth was determined by how many cattle he owned, and in the wake of Zuba's callous action, the headman and those with him put their hands to their heads, dropped to their knees and wailed. As Zuba stood smiling his smug smile, the headman, his hands clasped together as if he were praying, begged Zuba not to harm any more of the village livestock. Zuba helped the man to his feet and resumed their previous conversation. This time, the headman nodded agreeably, and soon beckoned a young villager to join them.

Zuba handed the AK-47 to the startled young man and pointed to the wooden boat tied to the jetty. 'Shoot, my friend.'

Zuba seemed to be perfectly aware that the villager could turn the gun on him, but with Zuba's soldiers training their weapons on the men cowering in front of the rebel leader, he also knew that the young man would not make such a fatal mistake. Reluctantly, the young man held the assault rifle close against his right side as he aimed at the boat. He had clearly never used an AK-47 before. Lucky reckoned he had probably never fired a gun in his life.

'Shoot! Shoot!' Zuba urged, slapping the youth on the back.

The young man pulled the trigger, letting off a burst of fire. Bullets splashed into the water in front of the boat, but none hit its target.

Zuba's smiled disappeared in a flash. Fiercely, menacingly, he issued the youth with an order. 'I command you to fire at the boat!'

The youth fired again, this time riddling the boat

with bullets. This brought a delighted cheer from the older rebel troops.

Zuba, satisfied, yanked the rifle from the villager's hands and handed it back to its owner. The boat, meanwhile, slowly sank at its moorings. Zuba then took a document from his tunic pocket and handed it to the young man, giving him detailed instructions. The young man nodded gravely, then, taking the document with him, ran to the beach. Lucky and the rangers watched as he pushed one of the small boats through the low breaking waves and out into deeper water.

Climbing into the boat, the young man took a seat in the stern, his weight sending the bow into the air. Starting the boat's small outboard motor, he turned the boat around, and with the engine buzzing like a mosquito, he headed out onto the lake and turned east.

'What is he doing, I wonder,' said Julius.

'Mwanza lies to the east,' said Lucky. 'I reckon he's delivering a message for Zuba.' He had a pretty good idea what that message was. The document that Zuba handed to the messenger had looked very much to Lucky like the letter he'd earlier written at Zuba's command – a letter which stated that Lucky and his rangers would be released unharmed when a ransom of one million dollars was paid.

Now Chawinga came toward the prisoners, beckoning them. 'Come to the jetty, all of you.'

'Where are you taking us now?' Lucky demanded. One of the guards pushed him forward.

'We are all going for a little boat ride,' Chawinga replied with a chuckle.

Major Jinko stood on the *Canberra*'s bridge to watch the Heron make a night landing. Away to the north, with its navigation lights winking, the Heron banked tightly and made its final approach to *Canberra*. The big ship, with the *Julius Nyere* scudding along at its side, had reversed its course once it drew level with the border between Tanzania and Kenya, and was now steaming south along the Tanzanian coast, with Pemba Island on its left. The rays from the rising moon lit a golden path across a calm Indian Ocean. On the *Canberra*'s flight deck, lines of small lights, which looked like precise rows of fireflies, marked out the UAV's flight path.

Although Herons weren't designed for landing on ships, Jinko had kept the Bluey over northwest Tanzania, between Leboo and the Burundi border, for as long as he could. He had been hoping to find a trace of Colonel Zuba and Lucky. Jinko had only given his approval for the drone to return to the ship when its fuel gauge indicated that it must come back to refuel – or crash. Hour after hour, the Heron's cameras had scoured the landscape of northwest Tanzania. When darkness fell, its infrared camera had been switched on. Yet, while the UAV had spotted plenty of Tanzanians on the ground, none had looked like the people Jinko was looking for.

He watched as the Heron made a perfect landing, piloted remotely from the operations centre. Like ants converging on food, deck crew swarmed around the UAV, and it was soon wheeled to the nearest deck lift.

'Well, that was a waste of time,' said Lieutenant Commander Lockhart, from beside Major Jinko.

'I know,' Jinko replied with a sigh, turning from the angled bridge window. 'I got it wrong. I let Zuba outfox us. You know, I don't think he went west after all. That was the easy option.'

'So, where is he?'

'He could have gone south, back into the game reserve. Or east, toward Mount Kilimanjaro. Or north toward Lake Victoria. From here on, I think I'm going to have to rely on gut instinct to track down Colonel Zuba.'

'Gut instinct?' Lockhart smirked. 'Very scientific. And what does your gut tell you, Major?'

Jinko rubbed his chin. 'North. My gut says he went north. Toward the lake.'

The battered blue landing craft carried Zuba's little army, complete with Land Rovers and trail bikes, to a small island in Lake Victoria. The long, narrow island, about the size of three tennis courts placed end to end, rose up to a small hillock that reached twenty metres at its highest. This, and other neighbouring islands, formed part of a national park. There were a few scattered trees as well as several huts that had been illegally built by the lake fisherman to provide shelter during storms. With no permanent residents, the island was deserted when the landing craft arrived and disgorged its passengers.

Zuba's men quickly hid their vehicles under the trees, covering them with green camouflage netting taken from the Tanzanian Army and peppering it with branches. Once this was done, most of the rebel soldiers set about casting string baited with pieces of goat meat into the lake. The captives were assigned to one of the fishermen's huts, and as the surrounding waters of the lake acted like a wall, Zuba allowed them to sit outside and watch the soldiers attempt to fish.

'What are you trying to catch?' Lucky called to Chawinga, who stood close by with a line in his hand.

'Nile perch,' replied Zuba's deputy, looking around at Lucky. 'This a nice fish, with very tasty white flesh.' He smiled, revealing gaps in his teeth. 'When you catch one, that is. These fish, they don't like goat meat as much as we do.'

Chawinga was right, the fish didn't bite. When the sun began to set, he gave up on trying to catch perch for dinner and lit a cooking fire. Two large iron pots hung on a metal bar over the flames. One pot contained a stew made from the last of the goat meat, which would feed Zuba, Chawinga and one or two favoured soldiers. For the rest, Chawinga prepared the RAT's staple of bean soup.

The prisoners were made to sit and eat their dinner on one side of the cooking fire, while Zuba's men did the same on the other side. Zuba, Chawinga, and Tonkei and Sirum – the two older men who usually guarded the prisoners – sat together in a separate group, eating goat stew. A new recruit and an older boy soldier watched over Lucky and his rangers, with AK-47s cradled uncomfortably in their hands.

'What's your name, son?' Lucky asked the recruit

standing guard. When the boy failed to reply, Lucky smiled. 'There's nothing to be afraid of. No one is going to harm you. What's your name?'

'It is Legeny, sir,' the boy replied in a faint voice, before looking away.

'You should not call him "sir"!' the other youth admonished.

The boy only shrugged in response to this.

'Where are you from, Legeny?' Lucky asked. 'Which village?'

'Mdinga,' the boy replied.

'And how old are you?'

'Eleven, sir.'

'Would you like to go home to your mother, Legeny, and stop being a soldier?'

Legeny nodded, and seemed close to bursting into tears. 'Yes, sir.'

'You should not talk with him, Legeny!' the older boy said angrily. 'Be quiet.' Coming closer, he took the youngster roughly by the arm and dragged him away, forcing him to sit by the water, where he cradled his AK-47 in his lap and cried quietly to himself.

When the older guard was not looking, Lucky managed to catch Legeny's eye and smiled at him. Legeny wiped his eyes with the back of his hand and shyly smiled back. Quickly, he turned away so that his older comrade didn't see the smile.

Ben, Caesar and their party landed back at Leboo by Seahawk. Lieutenant Roy's men had set up a tented camp inside one of the village goat compounds, which was surrounded by a wooden palisade protecting them from lions and hyenas roaming in the night. The Tanzanian soldiers had been joined in the cramped encampment by the GRRR men. And here, sitting around a camp fire, with bemused village goats pressing in around them, Ben, Baz, Chris and Sergeant Simma reported the outcome of their Dar es Salaam trip to the entire team.

'So, how did you hit the jackpot on the docks?' Charlie asked Ben. As he spoke, Charlie removed one of his Zoomers to check the knee mechanism. None of the other GRRR men as much as blinked at the sight, but the eyes of half-a-dozen astonished Tanzanian soldiers stood out on stalks.

'We just kept searching, and had almost called it a day when we discovered the ivory in the last container we opened,' Ben replied, ruffling his EDD's neck. 'Isn't that right, Caesar? You found it in the last one.'

At the mention of his name, Caesar's tail began to wag.

'And what happened to the ivory shipment, Fulton?'

asked Duke Hazard. He was lying back with his hands behind his head, chewing gum.

Ben grinned. 'We burned the entire load right there on the dock.'

Baz chuckled. 'That'll send Zuba a message.'

'But will he get the message?' asked Tim McHenry.

At this, Lieutenant Roy spoke up. 'As soon as I heard of Sergeant Fulton's success, I radioed my superiors. The destruction of Zuba's ivory shipment will be reported in the news broadcasts of Tanzanian Government radio in the morning.'

'Assuming Zuba hears it, will he believe it?' said McHenry.

'Doesn't matter if he doesn't,' Charlie remarked. 'It's enough to put doubt in his mind and make him worry about where his next dollar is coming from. We're priming him for a meeting with our Japanese ivory merchant.' He glanced across the firelight at Toushi Harada. 'Right, Toushi?'

'I hope that I can meet your expectations, Sergeant Grover,' said Toushi. 'I have never before been involved in undercover work.'

'There's a first time for everything, mate,' said Baz. 'You'll be great.'

Mrs Isabella Corbett opened the door to find Nan, Josh and Maddie standing before her. 'Hello there,' she said, smiling warmly in recognition.

'Who's at the door, Bella?' came the gruff voice of her husband.

'It's Mrs Fulton, with Josh and Maddie,' Mrs Corbett called back over her shoulder.

This brought an alarmed response from Mr Corbett. 'I'm not here!' he shouted, before slamming the bedroom door.

Now it was Nan's turn to smile. 'I wanted to talk to you about Kelvin. I'm afraid that –'

'I know – he didn't turn up for the course with Josh and Sergeant Kasula today. Kelvin wasn't even sly enough to pretend he was still doing the course. He just wouldn't get out of bed this morning, claiming he was sick. I am a nurse, Mrs Fulton, and it was as obvious as the nose on my face that my son was not sick. But he still refused to get out of bed.'

'We did have an agreement, Mrs Corbett,' said Nan.

Kelvin's mother nodded. 'And we still do. Kelvin will be at the next class, don't you worry.'

'Good, and so will Josh. Right?' Nan put her hand on Josh's shoulder.

'Yes, Nan,' Josh replied with a sigh.

'Good on you, Joshie,' said Maddie, proud of her brother.

In Sunday's early morning light, Captain Chawinga led the RAT in a marching drill along the beach. To Lucky and the other prisoners, the drill was so slack it was laughable. The existing soldiers had only a rudimentary idea of how to march in step, while none of the seven new recruits seemed to know his left foot from his right. Worse still, several of them would turn the wrong way every time Chawinga gave the line of marchers the order to face in the opposite direction.

Zuba himself was to be found sitting out of the sun, beneath a tree, with his transistor radio held up to his ear.

'No!' he suddenly cried in disbelief. Zuba had just heard a news story that had chilled him to his core. According to the BBC, the Tanzanian Government was reporting that a large ivory shipment – believed to have come from ivory-poaching revolutionary Abraham Zuba – had been discovered and destroyed on the dock at Dar es Salaam. 'No! No! No!' Zuba raged. Jumping to his feet, he threw down his radio and agitatedly paced back and forth, muttering to himself.

Seeing this, Chawinga dismissed his troops and came hurrying over to Zuba. 'Colonel, what is the matter?'

Zuba stopped his pacing. 'Chawinga, the BBC – it says that our last ivory shipment was intercepted and destroyed!' He threw his hands in the air. 'This is the first time that one of our shipments has been found. Someone must have betrayed us. We are ruined!'

Chawinga nodded, taking in the news calmly. 'Do you believe the BBC? They could have made it up.'

'The BBC never lies, Chawinga,' Zuba returned, his eyes ablaze. 'Never! Do you realise what this means? We will have no money. No money! We will have to hunt elephants again. But that will take months – the hunting, the shipping, the waiting for payment from China. How will the Revolutionary Army of Tanzania survive in the meantime?'

'We should check with our contact at the docks, Colonel. We should check with Mr Zhu, just to make sure there is no mistake.'

'A mistake?' This thought seemed to calm Zuba. 'Yes. Do that, Chawinga. Contact Mr Zhu – at once.'

Chawinga hurried away to get on the RAT's VHF radio. As he did, Zuba noticed for the first time that Lucky and the other prisoners had been witness to all this. Sliding the pistol from the holster on his hip, he strode angrily toward the group of seated prisoners.

'Get them inside their hut!' he ordered the guards, waving the pistol around as he spoke. 'No more privileges for them. No more privileges!'

Lucky and his companions were hastily bundled into the small, windowless fisherman's hut. Behind them, the corrugated iron door was slammed shut and padlocked.

Through a gap in the wall, Lucky watched Zuba. It occurred to Lucky that the seizure of the ivory at the docks was no random act. When he had started work at the Wildlife Service, Chief Ranger Springer had told him that the dock authorities at Dar es Salaam rarely intercepted outgoing ivory. Maybe, just maybe, Lucky told himself, the Tanzanian Government had received some outside help to find this particular ivory shipment.

Lucky watched as Chawinga came hurrying back to Zuba. 'Colonel, I have spoken on the radio with Mr Zhu,' the RAT captain reported breathlessly. 'He say no mistake was made.'

Zuba groaned. 'No mistake?'

'He say that foreign soldiers searched the containers on the docks.'

'Foreign soldiers?'

'He say they had the help of a special dog.'

'A dog?' Zuba echoed, incredulous.

'It is true. A large brown dog. He said it was a war dog, Colonel.'

Inside the hut, Lucky smiled to himself. He had a very good idea who that large brown war dog was. And he guessed from this information that his friends from the GRRR were not far away.

'A war dog?' said Zuba. 'What is a war dog?'

Little did Zuba know that he would soon find out what a war dog was.

CHAPTER 14

In their restricted camp at Leboo, the men of the GRRR team sat under the shade of the plane trees that fringed the goat compound. Bored and frustrated, most of them were cleaning their weapons as they waited for intelligence on their target's location. Until they knew the whereabouts of Zuba and the hostages, they could do nothing and they could go nowhere.

Even Caesar was bored. He was lying on the dry earth beside Ben, who was studying his waterproof operational map. Caesar rested his jaw on the ground and closed his eyes. He was almost asleep when he felt something land on his nose. Opening his eyes, he saw a wasp sitting there, looking right back at him. Caesar was reminded of the time he had poked his nose into a beehive and was stung several times. The wasp looked just like those bees. It tickled his ultra-sensitive nose, and Caesar sneezed, sending the wasp and a puff of dust into the air. Caesar didn't close his eyes again. He remained alert, keeping a watch for more wasps.

It was now that the team had a stroke of luck. Lieutenant Roy strolled into the compound. 'There was an amusing piece of news on my radio, Ranger Springer, Sergeant Grover. The police at Mwanza have arrested a young man carrying what he purports to be a letter from Ranger Lucky Mertz.'

'Mwanza?' said Charlie, as he and Wallace Springer came to their feet. 'That's in the north, on the lake, isn't it?'

Springer nodded. 'At the southern end of Lake Victoria. It's the second largest city in Tanzania.'

'This letter will, of course, prove to be a forgery,' Roy said authoritatively. He chuckled to himself. 'What would the hostages be doing up there at Mwanza? I would wager a large sum that Zuba is skulking across the border in Burundi, or even in Rwanda, further north.'

But Charlie knew that every morsel of information was important. He turned to signaller Brian Cisco. 'Get me Papa.' Charlie then looked down at Ben. 'Can I have a look at that map, mate?'

Ben stood up and handed his map to Charlie. The two of them stood together and consulted the map, taking note of the grid reference that covered Mwanza. The sudden activity brought Caesar to a sitting position, and he looked up expectantly at his two best friends. There was a look on Caesar's face that seemed to say, *Are we going to play now?*

Before long, Cisco had contacted Major Jinko aboard *Canberra*. 'I got Papa for you, Charlie,' he announced, holding the handset of his VHF radio out to him.

Charlie took the handset. 'Papa, this is Oscar Zulu One. Do you copy? Over.'

'Roger that, Oscar Zulu One,' Jinko's voice came back over the air. 'Go ahead. Over.'

'Papa, we have local police intel that Game Boy could be in the vicinity of grid reference X-ray Four. Would that gel with your way of thinking? Over.'

There was a pause as Jinko consulted his own map. 'Oscar Zulu One, that gels with me.' This intelligence backed up Jinko's hunch that Zuba had gone north to Lake Victoria. 'Investigate in force. I say again, investigate in force. I'll send a Sally to give you a ride. Do you copy? Over.'

'Copy that, Papa. Oscar Zulu will investigate in force. Oscar Zulu out.'

Sally One collected the six-member party from Leboo for the flight up to Lake Victoria. Charlie was in charge for this Mwanza reconnaissance, accompanied by Ben and Caesar as well as Baz, Chris Banner, Casper Mortenson, and the Tanzanian Army's Lieutenant Roy.

The city of Mwanza was sprawled around several low

hills on Lake Victoria's southern shore, where a deep cove served as a port for ferries and other vessels working on the lake. Mwanza had a population of 700,000, yet most of the city's buildings were single-storeyed, many of them with mud walls. Downtown, there were a few concrete office buildings and hotels of four or five storeys. Using his GPS to locate Mwanza's police headquarters on Kenyatta Road, near the gate to the ferry port, the Sally's pilot set his helicopter down on vacant land almost directly opposite the building. A crowd of locals, many of them children, quickly gathered to gawk at the sleek military chopper and its passengers.

Charlie led the detachment out of the Seahawk and up the dusty steps, into the large shady foyer of the simple white concrete building. Half-a-dozen local policemen were lounging around the foyer when the soldiers walked in. All conversation terminated abruptly as the policemen turned to survey the heavily armed foreign troops with a mixture of suspicion and fear.

'What do you want here?' demanded a massive police sergeant stationed at the front desk.

'Who's in charge?' asked Charlie, walking up to the desk.

'Superintendent Welle is in charge.'

'Then we're here to see Superintendent Welle.'

'He is a very busy man.' The sergeant folded his arms over his huge stomach.

'So are we,' Charlie retorted. 'Men's lives are at stake. So, where do we find the superintendent, Sergeant?'

'Please do as he says,' said Lieutenant Roy, coming to join Charlie. 'These men are on important United Nations business sanctioned by our government.'

'You have no authority here,' the sergeant growled at Roy.

Chris Banner leaned across the desk. 'Trust me, man, you don't want us to have to go find your superintendent.'

'And you don't want to have to find a new job. Do you, mate?' added Baz.

The police sergeant glanced at the M-16 on the towering West Indian's shoulder, then at Baz as he cradled his Minimi like a favoured pet. The sergeant sighed. 'Wait a moment.' He turned away from the GRRR men, took up a telephone and spoke into the mouthpiece urgently. Replacing the receiver, he regarded Charlie sourly, then said, 'Follow me.'

The sergeant led the way across the foyer toward a distant corridor. Charlie and the others set off after him, with Baz bringing up the rear, walking backwards to keep an eye on the policemen in the foyer.

They had reached the corridor when the sergeant noticed Caesar padding along at Ben's side. 'That dog cannot be here,' he declared, stopping in his tracks. 'Dogs belong in the street.'

'That's not any dog,' declared Baz, sounding insulted. 'That's Caesar.'

'Where we go, Caesar goes,' Charlie said in a no-nonsense tone. 'Lead on, my friend.' He pointed down the corridor. 'Time is precious!'

With a grunt, the sergeant led the party into a spacious office. Behind a broad desk with little adornment, a short, tubby man was sitting eating ice-cream from a bowl. Wiping his mouth slowly with a napkin, he came to his feet.

'These are they, Superintendent Welle, sir,' the sergeant said apologetically. 'These are the United Nations people.'

Superintendent Welle frowned. 'What can I do for you, gentlemen? The Commissioner rang me from the capital to warn me that you would be coming to Mwanza, but I must confess I did not expect you quite so soon.'

'Sir, you arrested a person carrying a letter written by Lucky Mertz, the kidnapped Deputy Chief Ranger of the Tanzanian Wildlife Service,' said Charlie.

'Indeed.' Welle nodded, before self-consciously dabbing his lips with his napkin. 'Of course, the document was a forgery. This fellow was clearly trying to use it to obtain money by false pretences.'

'How do you know it was a forgery?' asked Baz.

'The very nature of it cried forgery!' the superintendent responded, waving around his napkin. 'And how and where would such a humble fellow obtain such a document? He has no known connection with Colonel Pink Eye and the Revolutionary Army of Tanzania.'

'Do you still have the letter, sir?' Ben asked. Caesar sat down to watch the scene unfold, his head cocked to one side with curiosity.

'Yes, of course I have the letter. It is evidence that will be introduced at court when the fellow is sent to trial.'

'May we see it, sir?' Charlie asked.

'Oh, very well,' Welle replied impatiently. He opened a drawer and took out the letter. It was a single page, folded and soiled. 'But it is clearly a forgery.'

As Charlie unfolded the letter, Baz and Ben also moved in to read it.

To the governments of Tanzania, Australia and New Zealand,

My men and I are safe and in good health. We are well cared for by Colonel Abraham Zuba and the Revolutionary Army of Tanzania. However, Colonel Zuba's patience is running out. He has instructed me to tell the Government of Tanzania that he has increased his demands for our release. Those demands are as follows:

The Tanzanian Government will guarantee in writing to refrain from all attempts to locate and arrest Colonel Zuba and his men in the future.

On payment of a ransom of US$1 million dollars,
my rangers and I will be released unharmed. How
and when that ransom is to be paid will be commu-
nicated in my next communication.
    The bearer of this letter must be paid one thou-
sand dollar.

                                              Lucky Mertz

'You see,' said Welle. 'Clearly, a very amateur attempt
to extort a thousand dollars. Or, "one thousand dollar"
as he has written there.'

'Well, mate,' said Baz, 'I've got news for you – this *is*
Lucky Mertz's signature.'

'And this is Lucky's handwriting,' Ben added, tapping
the letter in Charlie's hand.

A look of disbelief came over Superintendent Welle's
face. 'How can you be so sure?'

'Mate,' said Baz, 'you're looking at Lucky Mertz's three
best friends.'

This temporarily silenced Welle. Charlie peered
closely at the final demand. 'This request for a thousand
dollars up-front – that wasn't written by Lucky.'

'It's someone else's handwriting,' Ben agreed.
'Someone has squeezed it in, trying to copy Lucky's
handwriting.'

'He even used a different pen,' Baz added. 'Look, it's

just a slightly different shade of blue. But the first part is genuine. Trust me, it was written by Lucky Mertz.'

'Looks like the bloke carrying the letter decided to make himself a thousand bucks,' Charlie surmised. 'Where is he? Have you got him under lock and key, Superintendent?'

'He was injured in the scuffle to affect his arrest. He is at the hospital. But do not worry. On my orders, he is handcuffed to the bed so that he cannot escape.'

'Please take us to him right now,' said Charlie, handing the letter back to Welle. 'We need to find out where he came by this letter.'

'Very well. I will take you to the hospital myself,' said Welle, reaching for his peaked cap.

'Why is our prisoner being kept in the children's ward?' demanded Superintendent Welle.

'The other wards are all full,' explained Dr Patel, the Chief of Paediatrics at the Northern Medical Centre. Nervously he pushed his glasses up his nose. The doctor was not used to having armed soldiers in his hospital. 'He is little more than a boy, anyway.'

Superintendent Welle opened the door to the ward. 'If you please, Dr Patel. Kindly lead my United Nations colleagues and myself to the prisoner.'

'Very well.' The doctor turned to take the lead. 'He will be transferred to an adult ward as soon as there is a vacant bed. The hospital is so very, very busy.' He glanced at the carbine on Charlie's shoulder. 'I hope that you gentlemen will not be here long – guns and hospitals are not a good combination.'

'We'll get out of your way as soon as we've spoken with your patient, Doctor,' Charlie assured him. 'Our object is to save lives – the lives of the hostages being held by the RAT. Your patient could have vital information that will lead us to those hostages.'

'Just be as quick as you can, Sergeant,' Dr Patel said with a sigh.

'Roger to that, sir.'

In pairs, the men made their way through the children's ward, with Superintendent Welle bringing up the rear. It was a long, stark white room of a hundred beds – fifty down one side, fifty down the other – and a broad aisle separating them. Every bed was occupied. It was lunchtime, and the patients were being delivered their lunch by blue-uniformed nurses. Some of the children were too ill to feed themselves, and the nurses were spooning food into their mouths. Their meal appeared to consist of bowls of mashed banana.

'What are the children given to eat, Doctor?' Ben asked as they passed the pale and bandaged youngsters.

The patients eyed the visitors with awe, while the nurses frowned at the sight of their weapons.

'*Matoke*,' Dr Patel replied.

'And what is *matoke*?'

'Cooked green bananas.'

'Bananas?' queried Baz, who was walking directly behind Ben and Caesar. 'Is that very wholesome?'

'I assure you, it is most nutritious,' said the doctor. '*Matoke* is what most people in this country eat. In addition to *matoke*, once a week we are able to give the children a meal of maize and millet with beans, or sometimes with a little fish or red meat. This provides a balanced and more than adequate diet.'

Ben glanced at a boy hungrily scooping the last of the contents of his bowl. 'Their bowls don't appear to be that full,' he remarked.

'They get a lot more for dinner, at night, right?' said Baz.

'Er, no. Lunch is the most substantial meal of the day in Tanzania,' Dr Patel replied. 'The evening meal for these children will be a little bean soup and a mango-orange drink. At Christmas and other holiday times, they will be given date nut bread or sweet potato pudding as a special treat. You must remember that, when they leave the hospital and go home, these children may not be fed as much as they are here. Most of their families are very, very poor.'

When the group arrived at the very last bed in the ward, they found a young man lying on top of the blankets, fully clothed. His right wrist was handcuffed to the side of the bed. His face was badly bruised, and one eye had almost closed over.

'Why isn't he actually in the bed, Doctor?' Charlie asked, as they all stood around the bed looking at the young man.

'As I said, he is due to be transferred to an adult ward at any time. There is no point soiling a bed here in that circumstance.'

Lieutenant Roy scowled at the young man. 'What is your name?' he demanded.

The young man looked anxiously around the faces, and smiled weakly. 'Do not hit me, please! The policemen, they hit me.'

'You resisted arrest,' said Superintendent Welle.

'No one is going to hit you here,' Dr Patel assured the handcuffed youth. 'Tell these people your name.'

'Benjamin Kananga,' he answered warily.

'Where are you from?' asked Charlie.

Benjamin's eyes flashed to the Australian sergeant. 'My village is Ugali.'

'Ugali is west of here,' Lieutenant Roy explained to the foreigners.

'A village on the lake shore,' added Dr Patel.

'On the lake?' Charlie looked at Benjamin. 'Who gave you that letter you were carrying?' he asked.

Benjamin didn't hesitate to answer. 'Colonel Zuba,' he said.

'How can we be sure of that?' said Superintendent Welle.

Benjamin shrugged. 'It was him. I have seen him before.'

'And what did Colonel Zuba tell you to do with the letter?' Charlie continued.

'He said I should take it to the government radio station here in Mwanza, and tell them to put it on the air. They made me wait, and the next thing I know, the police arrive.'

'Where did Zuba give you the letter?' Charlie asked. Always calm, his tone of voice did not reveal Charlie's hope that the team was at last close to tracking Lucky down.

'At my village. At Ugali.'

'Was Ranger Lucky Mertz there?'

'There was a *mzungu* with yellow hair, and some rangers. They were all prisoners of Colonel Zuba.'

'And how many men did Zuba have with him?' Charlie asked.

'Many men and boys with guns. Perhaps fifty, perhaps a hundred.'

'And are they still at your village?'

Benjamin shrugged. 'I do not know. They were there when I came here to Mwanza.'

Charlie looked at the others and stroked his chin pensively. 'I think we have to believe this bloke.'

'I still do not think this boy has had anything to do with Zuba!' Superintendent Welle exclaimed. 'At best, this has been an attempt to waste our time. At worst, this has all been fabricated by this fellow in an attempt to obtain money for himself.'

'It was Colonel Zuba who gave me the letter to deliver, I swear!' Benjamin protested. 'He even gave me a gun and made me shoot it.'

Ben, who was standing at the end of the bed, intervened. 'Are these the same clothes Benjamin was wearing when he was arrested?' he asked the superintendent.

'I believe so, yes,' Welle replied with a frown.

Ben turned to Dr Patel. 'His clothes haven't been washed here by the hospital, Doctor?'

'No, no, they have not left his body.'

Ben turned to Benjamin. 'Show me how you held the gun, when Colonel Zuba made you fire it.'

Benjamin sat up as best he could, and with his left free arm, he attempted to mime holding the AK-47 against his side. Then he made a sound to imitate the sound of the firing of the assault rifle. 'Brrrrrrrr!'

'Are you left-handed or right-handed?' asked Ben.

Benjamin frowned. 'I am right-handed. Why?'

Ben nodded to himself. 'Okay. Everyone step away from the bed.'

'Do as he says,' Charlie instructed. He had worked with Ben long enough to never question his judgement while on ops.

As the doctor, the superintendent, the lieutenant and the rest of the GRRR party stepped back, Ben dropped to one knee in front of Caesar, who stood patiently at his side. Ben unclipped the EDD's leash and pointed to the youth on the bed. 'Caesar, seek on!'

Caesar padded to the side of the bed and put his nose over the edge to within a few centimetres of the youth. He sniffed Benjamin's right side and then eased his rear end onto the floor. There he sat, staring intently at the young man.

'What is the dog doing?' said Benjamin.

Charlie smiled. 'That, my friend, is Caesar's signature.'

'His what?' said Superintendent Welle.

'Caesar has picked up the scent of explosives,' Ben explained. 'As I suspected, Benjamin has gunshot residue on his clothes. I believe his story. I think that Zuba did genuinely send him here with the letter from Lucky.' Dropping to one knee, Ben pulled the labrador's head into a cuddle and patted his side. 'Well done, Caesar! Well done, mate!'

In response, Caesar wagged his tail with delight and licked Ben on the cheek, before returning his intense gaze to young Benjamin.

'So, Zuba was at Ugali,' said Charlie.

'And he may still be there,' Casper Mortenson remarked. 'With Lucky and the other hostages.'

Charlie nodded. 'We might have to pay a visit to Ugali. The rest of you stay here while I get on secure comms with Papa.'

Taking Superintendent Welle and Chris Banner with him, Charlie quickly departed for the police headquarters.

While the GRRR men were waiting at the hospital, they spoke with the young patients, trying to put them at ease and cheer them up. Baz proved particularly adept at getting smiles out of the children – he didn't have to say a word; he just pulled faces. Caesar was the most popular visitor, with the youngsters eager to pat him. Caesar greeted them with a wagging tail, often licking their outstretched hands, which brought giggles of pleasure. Ben noticed one particular boy of twelve or thirteen who was lying in his bed and looking at the ceiling, taking no interest in what was going on around him. He seemed impervious to the laughter and squeals of delight that were coming from his fellow patients.

'What's wrong with that young bloke?' Ben asked Dr Patel, pointing to the boy.

'That one has no physical ailment or injury,' the doctor replied. 'His is a very, very sad case. He saw his parents drown during a storm on the lake, after which he was forced to become a soldier in the Revolutionary Army of Tanzania. Somehow, he succeeded in escaping the clutches of Colonel Zuba and his men. He was found wandering aimlessly before he was brought here to the hospital. He has not spoken a word since he arrived. And if we do not feed him, he will not feed himself. The boy simply lies there, day in, day out. He is traumatised, and I am afraid there is no form of treatment that we can give him for that.'

'What's his name?' asked Ben.

The doctor consulted a list of patients. 'This boy is called Ephrem.'

Leading Caesar to the youngster's bedside, Ben encouraged the labrador to put his front paws up on the bed. 'Caesar, say hello to Ephrem.'

Caesar looked at Ben for a moment, as if to say, *What's wrong with this boy, boss?* Then he nuzzled young Ephrem with his nose, emitting a concerned whine as he did. When there was no reaction from the boy, Caesar put his front paws on the side of the bed. He then reached out and touched the boy's arm with his right paw, letting out another whine.

Slowly, Ephrem's head turned and his eyes fell on the labrador. Caesar licked the back of his hand. 'Nice dog,' he said softly. And then he began to gently stroke Caesar's head.

'He spoke!' exclaimed Dr Patel. 'The boy spoke! That is amazing! Not in a month has this boy said a word. It has taken your dog to open his mouth.'

Ben smiled. 'I'm not surprised. There's a hospital in western Sydney that uses specially trained dogs as hospital visitors for children. The dogs do wonders for the spirits of sick kids, and have boosted their recovery times enormously. Look at Caesar – he knows that Ephrem isn't happy, and wants to help him.'

On hearing his name mentioned, Caesar looked around at Ben. He quickly returned his attention to Ephrem, who now managed a faint smile as he looked at the chocolate labrador.

'Quite amazing,' said Dr Patel, as he watched the interaction between dog and boy. 'If I had not seen it for myself, I would not have believed it.'

'There's an element of trust between children and dogs that seems to trigger this sort of reaction,' said Ben. 'Dogs don't judge us, they just love us. And as you can see, Doctor, dog therapy can be the best medicine.'

Charlie and Chris hurried to the Seahawk helicopter waiting across the road from the police headquarters.

Getting on the chopper's radio, Charlie called Major Jinko aboard *Canberra*.

'Papa, we have good reason to believe that Game Boy is, or was, at X-ray Two,' said Charlie. 'Permission for insertion at X-ray Two? Over.'

'Wait, Oscar Zulu One,' Jinko replied. After a pause, the major said, 'Oscar Zulu One, we have intercepted a military band VHF transmission from your area. We think it's from Bullseye, to a receiver named Zhu in the area of Kilo Twenty-four. Do you copy? Over.'

Charlie unfolded his operational map and pinpointed grid K24. That grid covered Dar es Salaam. 'Copy that, Papa. Zhu, at Kilo Twenty-four. Over.'

'The message was in plain English,' advised Jinko. 'The sender asked the receiver to confirm that the contraband shipment had been seized and destroyed, which he did. Over.'

Charlie smiled with satisfaction. 'Good. Bullseye will be desperate for dough now. Do we know who this receiver was? This Zhu character? Over.'

'Baz reports that Zhu is a Chinese port official at Kilo Twenty-four. Over.'

'Copy that. Where do we proceed from here? Over.'

'All Oscar Zulus will proceed to X-ray Two to locate Game Boy. Over.'

'By heelo? Over.'

'There's no time to send you Sally Two. Sally One

will collect Oscar Zulu Two and team.' Oscar Zulu Two was Sergeant Duke Hazard's codename. 'You and your people find yourselves a boat. Let me know your ETA at X-ray Two. Over.'

'Roger to that. Finding a boat. Over and out.'

Josh looked at Kelvin Corbett lying on the floor. Josh had just thrown him to the mat like a rag doll, and now Kelvin was crying.

'I'm sorry, Kelvin,' said Josh, sounding slightly exasperated. 'I'm only doing what Sergeant Kasula taught us to do.'

'Get up, Kelvin,' Sergeant Kasula instructed. 'Do what I've trained you to do. You've been bone lazy.'

'It's not fair!' Kelvin sobbed, dragging his knees up into his chest and refusing to budge. 'Everyone picks on me – my dad, my mum and the school.' He glared at Sergeant Kasula. '*You* too!'

'I don't pick on you, son,' Sergeant Kasula said with a sigh. 'You picked on Josh, remember? That's why you're here.'

'I hate being different from everyone else!' Kelvin blurted.

'Different?' said Sergeant Kasula. 'How are you different?'

'I'm taller than everyone in my class. I stand out.'

'Yes, but –'

'I'm a year older than everyone else in my class, too.'

'That's because you had to repeat a year,' said Josh.

'That was because I don't read all that good. And everyone stares at me and laughs at me. They think I'm stupid.'

'You're not stupid,' said Josh, sitting down beside Kelvin. 'But you've got to stop giving up all the time. Let's just do this. If you did what Sergeant Kasula taught us, you'd be throwing me, not the other way around. And we could all go home.'

Josh had been tempted to let Kelvin throw him a few times, just to get these sessions back on track, but something in him wouldn't let him do that. A voice in his head told him that Kelvin had to earn his successes.

Kelvin looked at him. 'I don't give up all the time!' he snivelled.

'Well, what are you doing now?'

'I'm . . . I'm . . .'

'Giving up,' said Josh.

'Okay,' said Sergeant Kasula. 'I'm sure as heck not giving up on you, Kelvin. But maybe I've been approaching this the wrong way. I've got an idea.' Reaching down, he offered Kelvin his hand. 'Let's try something different.'

As the prisoners sat in their hut, bathed in perspiration, they could hear the rumbling sound of a large boat engine growing nearer.

'Is that it, Ranger Lucky?' Koinet asked, sounding excited. 'Is that a boat bringing soldiers to rescue us?'

'I'm not sure, Koinet,' Lucky replied. He peered through a slit in the corrugated iron wall.

'You said that they would rescue us,' said Koinet, his voice full of hope. 'Now they have come, yes?'

But Lucky could see little, and learned nothing of what was happening.

Then came the sound of the hut door being unlocked. The door opened, and the two regular guards stood peering in at them.

'Out, rascal rangers,' said one. 'Out!'

When Lucky and his five companions emerged from their cramped quarters, they could see a vessel approaching the beach. This was no rescue craft. This was the aged blue landing craft that had brought them all to the island.

Tears began to roll down Koinet's cheeks. 'You said they would rescue us!' he wailed at Lucky. 'You said we would be able to go home to our families.'

'Keep quiet, Koinet!' old Julius urged. 'Say nothing of what Ranger Lucky told us.'

'Keep quiet yourself, old man!' Koinet snapped. 'I have had enough of all this. They will never let prisoners go home. They will kill you all.' He looked at the pair of sentinels. 'I wish to join you,' he said.

Both guards looked surprised. 'What do you mean?' asked the one named Sirum.

'I wish to become one of Colonel Zuba's soldiers.'

'Koinet, don't give up now!' said Lucky.

The young ranger looked at Lucky with a fierce gleam in his eyes. 'Can you give me a guarantee, Ranger Lucky, that we will be rescued?'

Lucky sighed. 'Koinet, you know I can't do that.'

Tonkei, the second guard, guffawed. 'No one will rescue you, boy.'

'It is as I thought,' said Koinet. 'Then I will be one of you.'

'You want to join the ranks of the RAT?' asked Sirum.

'Yes, if that will mean I am no longer a prisoner,' Koinet replied.

Sirum shrugged. 'If that is what you want. We will take you to Colonel Zuba, to see what he says. Any more of you want to become soldiers in the Revolutionary Army of Tanzania?'

185

The four other rangers looked at each other, and then at Lucky, before they all shook their heads.

'You come with me,' Sirum said, grasping Koinet by the arm and pulling him toward the door.

'Koinet, you are making a big mistake,' said Julius. He grabbed Koinet's other arm to prevent him from leaving.

A tug of war ensued as Sirum attempted to drag Koinet out by one arm and Julius tried to hold him back by the other. Tonkei stepped up and bashed Julius on the arm with the butt of his AK-47. Howling in pain, Julius let go of Koinet. Lucky leapt up to help Julius. In the scuffle that followed, Julius was pushed to the ground, and as Lucky bent to protect him, the butt of Sirum's AK-47 thudded into his skull. Lucky's hat went flying, and Lucky went down.

With Koinet removed from the hut, both guards levelled their weapons at the inmates.

'We will shoot if any of you try anything like that again!' Tonkei declared, partly scared, partly angry.

'Take it easy, take it easy!' said Lucky. Instinctively, he put his fingers to his head and felt the sticky blood in his hair.

Sirum picked up Lucky's akubra. Turning, he placed the hat on Koinet's head. 'There, now you wear the boss's hat,' he said, grinning.

As Tonkei slammed and locked the door and then

stood watch on the remaining prisoners, Sirum took hold of Koinet's shirt and led him toward Zuba, who was watching the landing craft as it ground on the beach and its front ramp was lowered to the sand.

Inside the hut, Roadga helped Lucky to his feet. 'Are you all right, Ranger Lucky?' he asked with concern.

'I'm fine, thanks. I've got a thick skull,' Lucky assured him, though he could feel the onset of a throbbing headache. He turned his attention to the oldest ranger. 'How about you, Julius? No broken bones?'

Julius, holding his injured arm, tried to put on a brave face. 'I do not think anything is broken,' he said. 'It is that stupid boy Koinet that I am worried about. He does not know what he has got himself into!'

Villagers at Ugali watched with idle curiosity as an unfamiliar fishing boat came chugging into their cove at twilight. Lieutenant Roy had commandeered it in Mwanza and was now at the wheel. Lying out of sight in the bottom of the wooden craft with other GRRR men, Charlie spoke into the personal radio attached to his bulletproof vest. 'All Oscar Zulus – go, go, go!'

In seconds, Charlie, Ben, Caesar, Chris and Casper rose up from where they had been hiding below the gunwales. They leapt over the sides and splashed through the shallows. Up the beach they ran, weapons ready for action.

At the same time, in a coordinated move, Duke Hazard and the remainder of the Operation Pink Elephant team, accompanied by Sergeant Simma, entered the village from the southern, inland side. They'd been dropped two kilometres from the village by Sally One and had walked the rest of the way. Otherwise, the sound of the chopper would have been heard in Ugali, alerting Zuba and his men if they'd been in the village. But a thorough search of the village found no sign of the RAT.

'All clear, Charlie,' said Sergeant Hazard, once the search was completed. 'No bad guys.'

'Okay.' Charlie shouldered his rifle. 'Let's see what the headman has to say.'

Lieutenant Roy now joined them, and, using the local dialect, he questioned the same headman whose cattle compound had been sprayed with bullets by Abraham Zuba. The headman was coy at first, but in the end, after much cajoling, he told Lieutenant Roy what he wanted to know.

'The headman says that Zuba, his men and the hostages are all out there.' Lieutenant Roy pointed to the lake's northern horizon. 'On an island.'

'Do you trust this guy?' said Hazard, nodding to the headman.

'Not entirely,' said Roy. 'But at the moment I think he is more frightened of us than he is of Zuba.'

'Then, to the island we go,' said Charlie. 'Bring the headman with us.'

Aboard *Canberra*, Major Jinko was trying to keep his temper. On the bridge, bathed in blue light, he was in the middle of a tense conversation with the air division commander, Lieutenant Commander Lockhart, as the other crewmen of the bridge pretended to look the other way.

'I need that drone over that island,' Jinko declared, stabbing the air with his index finger. 'I don't want my boys going in there blind.'

'And for the umpteenth time, Major, this ship is not certified for night take-offs of UAVs. I can't authorise it. Sorry, no can do.' Lockhart folded his arms.

'You landed the drone in the dark!' Jinko protested. 'Why can't you launch it in the dark?'

'That was different,' Lockhart came back, sounding increasingly exasperated. He turned to Captain Rixon, who sat in his command chair, looking at one of the monitors. 'Sir, tell the major that we can't launch the UAV,' he said, almost pleadingly.

Jinko looked at the skipper. 'Well, Captain?'

189

Captain Rixon sat back in his seat, stretched and sighed. 'Jinko, I'd like to help you and your men out, but Lockhart is right. We aren't certified for night UAV operations. It was not something the brass ever envisaged for *Canberra*.'

'But you let the drone land on the ship at night,' Jinko persisted.

'I had little choice other than to let it land,' Rixon replied with a helpless shrug. 'It was either try to land the thing, or ditch it on the drink after you kept it over northern Tanzania in darkness. I had to weigh the consequences of two choices – break the rules and land the UAV at night, something we'd never done before, or let the multi-million dollar Heron run out of fuel and fall into the Indian Ocean. I can live with the consequences of the first. The second could have cost me my command.'

'Lives may depend on that UAV being in position over my team, Captain,' said Jinko.

'I know. And we can launch it at first light – not before. If you want to land your men on that island tonight, you'll have to tell them to take extra precautions. But they'll be doing it without the help of the UAV.'

Darkness wrapped around the fishing boat as it eased toward the island which the Ugali headman had identified as Colonel Zuba's hide-out.

'Cut the engine,' Charlie ordered.

Sergeant Simma, at the boat's wheel, quickly did so. The boat glided to a stop and lay idly on the smooth surface of the lake. All was silent.

'Okay, Chris, Casper, do your thing,' Charlie said in a low voice.

Chris Banner and Casper Mortenson, both highly experienced divers, slipped over the side of the boat and into the water. Stripped down to black underpants, each man had a belt circling his waist, with a commando knife and a torch hanging from it. Swimming slowly to minimise noise, the pair made for the island. A hundred metres out from the beach, both men slid under the surface and swam the last leg underwater.

They emerged in the shallows, thirty metres apart, and advanced up the narrow strip of sand at a crouching run. Both drew their knives and, without making a sound, crept barefoot from one fishermen's shelter to another. They found the shelters empty. They searched the length and breadth of the island, but found no trace of Zuba, his men or the hostages.

'Nothing,' said Casper, shaking his head with disappointment. 'This could have been a red herring, Chris.'

'Maybe,' Chris replied. 'Maybe not.' He pointed to the

remains of a cooking fire in front of the huts, and made his way toward it. 'Someone has been here recently.' Squatting down, he put a hand over the cooking fire's embers. 'They're still warm, man! We haven't missed them by more than an hour or two.'

Taking the torch from his belt, he pointed it in the direction of the fishing boat moored off the island, and flashed a signal to Charlie in Morse code.

Charlie saw the blinking light and read the message aloud. 'No go,' he announced sourly. He called for Sergeant Simma to start the engine and steer the boat to the beach to collect Chris and Casper. Charlie then directed Brian to make contact with Major Jinko. Before long, as the boat got underway, Brian was handing Charlie the VHF handset.

'Papa, this is Oscar Zulu One,' Charlie said into the mouthpiece. 'The birds have flown. Do you copy? The birds have flown. Over.'

'Copy that, Oscar Zulu One,' Jinko replied, with disappointment obvious in his voice. 'Await further orders. Papa out.'

'Roger that. Oscar Zulu One out.'

Jinko, frustrated by the failure to locate the hostages at the island, decided to consult Major General Jones, his superior at SOCOM back in Australia. From *Canberra*'s communications room, he put in a radio telephone call to the general.

'Sir, they're not on the island. But they must have a boat. They could have landed anywhere around Lake Victoria.'

'Get that UAV airborne, Jinko,' General Jones instructed. 'You've got to find that boat.'

'The navy won't launch the UAV until daybreak, sir,' Jinko replied. 'And where do we look? Zuba could have gone back to the Tanzanian mainland, or across the lake to Uganda or Kenya to the north. Where do I send the UAV to look?'

'You're in charge if this op, Jinko,' said the general. 'It's your call. Just make the right one.'

In the night, Zuba had landed on Tanzania's northern lake coast. Unloading his vehicles from the landing craft, he had brought his soldiers and prisoners to a village on the plain on the northwest rim of the Kigosi Game Reserve. There was a large cattle compound at this village, with the usual wooden palisade fencing it in and protecting the occupants from marauding wild animals. In the middle of the compound sat a typical round wooden hut with a dirt floor and thatched roof. This was the hut of the herdsman whose job it was to look after the cattle, but on Zuba's instructions, his men had evicted the hut's occupants and installed Lucky and his rangers in it. This became their latest prison.

Before the door to the hut was padlocked, Zuba came to speak with his prisoners. He brought a sheepish Koinet with him. Still wearing Lucky's hat, Koinet stood beside the rebel leader in the open doorway. Behind the pair, several of Zuba's soldiers had their AK-47s at the ready.

Zuba produced his smug smile. 'Are there more of you rangers who wish to follow the wise example of brave Koinet here, and join the Revolutionary Army of Tanzania?'

The only response came from old Julius, who spat on the floor with contempt.

'No?' said Zuba, before laughing to himself. 'Tomorrow, perhaps. Or the next day.'

'It's not too late to change your mind, Koinet,' said Lucky. 'We won't hold it against you if you decide to rejoin us.'

'Koinet will not be changing his mind,' said Zuba, putting an arm around the young man's shoulders. 'Will you, boy?'

Koinet smiled weakly. 'No, Colonel.'

'You are now a brave soldier of the revolution.'

'Yes, Colonel.'

'So, Ranger Lucky,' said Zuba, 'I will be saying bye-bye to you for the time being. You rangers must stay here while my men and I go on a mission.'

'What kind of mission?' Lucky asked.

Zuba chuckled to himself. 'That is for me to know and you to find out, my friend.' He then motioned to the two regular guards to close and lock the door. 'But it will be a very profitable mission, I can assure you,' Zuba added.

The door closed, the chain rattled as the padlock was

snapped shut, and before long Lucky and his rangers heard the Land Rovers and motorcycles noisily depart the village. Lucky could see nothing from inside the hut, but from the direction of the receding sound of engines, he felt sure that Zuba and his men were heading south, into the game reserve.

As dawn broke over Lake Victoria, the fishing boat being used by the GRRR team sat with its bow on the sands of the little island. The men were eating their breakfast – cold MREs from their packs – on the beach. Using water from their canteens, they brewed tea and coffee at the fireplace last used by the men they were pursuing. While they waited on the beach, Major Jinko contacted Charlie by radio.

'Sit tight, Oscar Zulu One,' Jinko instructed. 'The sun is up, and so is Bluey. As soon as it spots anything, you'll have new orders. Papa out.'

'Roger to that,' replied Charlie. 'Oscar Zulu out.' Charlie handed the handset back to Brian Cisco.

'It's like hoping to win a lottery,' said Ben. He was sitting close by with Caesar lying full-length at his side.

'What is?' asked Charlie.

'Waiting for the drone to find Zuba.'

'Any better ideas?'

'What about the plan to use Toushi to lure Zuba into a trap?' Ben suggested.

'How do we make that work?'

'You mentioned a name before – Zhu. You know – the radio transmission to Dar es Salaam that was intercepted?'

'Yep. What about it?'

'It occurred to me earlier that Mr Zhu was the name of the Chinese port official who opened the containers for us – under protest.'

Charlie looked interested. 'And . . .?'

'We should get the Tanzanian police to have a word with Mr Zhu and set up a meeting between Toushi and the illustrious colonel.'

Charlie smiled. 'It's worth a try. Beats sitting on our rear ends all day.'

'Do you reckon the local cops could be persuasive enough?' said Baz. 'To get Mr Zhu to cooperate?'

'What if we got Wally Springer to pay Mr Zhu a visit?' Ben suggested. 'We could rely on Springer to be persuasive. He wants his rangers back, safe and well.'

'The chief ranger? It's worth a try,' said Charlie, thoughtfully. They had parted company with Chief Ranger Springer back at Leboo. 'Brian, get me Papa on the blower again.'

Mr Zhu sat fearfully in his office chair, eying the half-a-dozen Tanzanian policemen who stood watching him from across the room. One of the policemen was idly leaning against the wall and playing with a truncheon.

On the broad expanse of asphalt outside the dockside office, an RAN Seahawk had just set down, its rotors whirring. Contrary to what the pilot of Sally One had been told only a day earlier by port radio, there was plenty of room for a helicopter to land here. And now Sally One had done just that, having collected Chief Ranger Springer from Leboo and flown him down to Dar es Salaam.

Wasting no time, Springer strode through the office door and stood over the port official. 'You have a VHF radio, and you use it to maintain contact with Abraham Zuba, a wanted ivory poacher.'

'No! No!' Mr Zhu replied, violently shaking his head. 'This is not true!'

'Your conversation with Zuba, where you told him of the ivory shipment seized here yesterday, was intercepted by ASIA, the Australian Signals Intelligence Agency. We heard everything.'

'No, no, not true!' Mr Zhu protested. His brow had quickly become coated with perspiration. 'I know nothing. Nothing.'

Springer raised his eyebrows. 'You know nothing?' He paused for a moment. 'Do you have grandchildren,

Mr Zhu? You look the right age to have grandchildren.'

Mr Zhu looked perplexed. 'Yes, six grandchildren. Three boy, three girl. Why you ask?'

'Recently, the ivory exporting nations of the world jointly declared the illegal export of ivory a "serious crime". Do you know what that means, Mr Zhu? It means that now, when you are convicted of illegal ivory trafficking – and believe me, you will be convicted – you won't be sentenced to a year or two in prison. You will be sentenced to *life* in prison. And when I say life, I mean life! They will lock you in a squalid African prison and throw away the key. You will never bounce your grandchildren on your knee again, Mr Zhu.'

Mr Zhu paled. 'I . . . I am only a poor port official,' he stammered, dropping his eyes to the floor.

'Life in prison, Mr Zhu,' Springer reiterated. 'But if you were to cooperate with us – if you were to help us – I would recommend leniency to the court.'

Mr Zhu raised his eyes. 'Leniency?'

'Help us catch Zuba, and the government could be convinced to drop the more serious charges against you. Well, what's it to be? I don't have all day.'

'I . . .'

'The rest of your life in prison, or a lenient judge. You decide, Mr Zhu. Your fate is in your own hands, mate.'

The RAT convoy rolled across flat bushland, following a rough dirt track that wound around low grassy rises and past thin clumps of plane trees standing starkly on the plain. The second of the two Land Rovers began to flash its headlights at the first. This brought the first Land Rover to an abrupt stop, and the second Land Rover and all the trail bikes did the same.

Zuba stepped from the first vehicle and walked back to the second, to its open front passenger window. 'What is it, Chawinga?' he demanded irritably. 'Why the flashing lights?'

'I have just received a message on the radio, Colonel,' Chawinga replied, nodding to the VHF military radio sitting on the floor between his feet. 'From our good friend Zhu in Dar es Salaam.'

'And what did he have to say for himself?'

'He say that he has been approached by a Japanese ivory buyer who is prepared to pay fifteen hundred dollars for every kilo of ivory we supply.'

Zuba raised his eyebrows. 'Fifteen hundred a kilo? Really?'

'And to prove his good faith,' Chawinga went on, 'he is prepared to give us fifty thousand dollars in advance as a down payment. Or so he says.'

'He will give us fifty thousand dollars in advance?'

'This Japanese buyer is in Tanzania and is asking for a meeting with you personally, Colonel. He says that he will hand over the fifty thousand at the meeting.'

Zuba pursed his lips as he considered the proposition. 'The money would be very handy, Chawinga. But the meeting would have to be on our terms.'

'And on our territory,' Chawinga added.

Zuba nodded slowly. 'Call our good friend Zhu. Set up a meeting – here, in the game reserve. The Japanese buyer can fly in to meet us.'

'Oscar Zulu One, from Papa. Over.'

Brian Cisco passed the radio handset to Charlie.

'Oscar Zulu One receiving,' Charlie replied. 'Over.'

'Bullseye is in the game. I repeat, Bullseye is in the game. Do you copy? Over.'

Charlie smiled. 'Copy that, Papa. Over.' Sitting around him on the fishing boat, the other members of the team were also smiling – the message meant that Zuba had taken the bait and had agreed to a meeting with their fictitious Japanese ivory merchant.

'I'll give you the map reference for the RP he's specified,' said Major Jinko. 'It's an airstrip in a game reserve. Bullseye wants the meeting tomorrow at dawn. We'll have Bluey over the location shortly, and will insert the full team less one tonight using the Sallys. You'll be dropped ten clicks north of the RP and will have to yomp it in to the RP to be ready and waiting for Bullseye

201

at dawn. We'll organise a local light aircraft to deliver the bait. Over.'

'Roger to that, Papa. What's the map reference for the RP? Over.'

Jinko replied with the map reference for the rendez-vous point set by Zuba, then advised a time when two Seahawks from *Canberra* would rendezvous with the team at a mainland beach. There, the team was to board the helicopters for the flight south to the Kigosi Game Reserve. The plan was for the GRRR team to be deposited ten kilometres north of the location nominated by Zuba, and travel the rest of the way on foot to be in position for the dawn meeting, where they would ambush the RAT commander. 'And the codename for the bait is Sinker,' he added. 'Over.'

Charlie finished marking the map references for the insertion point and the location of the meeting with Zuba. 'Copy that, Papa. Do we know if Game Boy is with Bullseye? Over.'

'Negative, Oscar Zulu One. We have no intel on the location of Game Boy. He could be with Bullseye, so proceed with caution tomorrow. We want no collateral damage. Papa out for now.'

'Roger to that, Papa. Oscar Zulu One out.' Charlie turned to the others. 'Let's get this old crate moving. We have an appointment with Colonel Zuba.'

As dawn was breaking in the direction of the Indian Ocean, a high-winged, single-engine Cessna 172 aircraft appeared from the northeast.

'There's Toushi's plane,' said Baz, pointing to the Cessna, which was slowly descending as it drew nearer.

'Yes, but where's Zuba?' Charlie peered through his binoculars, sweeping the surrounding area.

The GRRR team, less Toushi Harada, had reached the area on foot the night before. Once they had assured themselves that neither Zuba nor his men were in the vicinity, the team had dug in along the southern side of a rough airstrip on the plain. The men were spread out in a line, hidden in long grass, with their weapons ready. Several hundred metres behind them, one of the country's few sealed highways, the B3, ran thin, flat and deserted across a northern tip of the Kigosi Game Reserve.

One of the Sallys had flown Toushi Harada to the town of Ushirombo, which sat just to the east of the game reserve. There, Toushi had hurriedly purchased and donned civilian clothes, and in the lead-up to sunrise, he'd boarded the Cessna 172 at the local airfield. The plane had been chartered for him by the Tanzanian Government at the hurried request of Major Jinko via SOCOM.

Brian Cisco had Major Jinko on the radio, and he now handed the handset to Charlie.

'Sinker is in sight, Papa,' Charlie reported. 'But no sign of Bullseye. Over.'

'Copy that.'

The Cessna eased lower in the sky as it approached, and then it was on the ground and running quickly along the dirt strip on its three wheels. At the far end, it slowed, before turning around to face the wind, ready to take off again. The passenger door opened and out stepped Toushi, adorned in shorts and a bright floral shirt, carrying a bulging backpack by the straps. There he stood, beside the aircraft, looking around uncertainly for someone to appear. But in all directions there was no movement, no sound.

From his position in the grass, Charlie kept his binoculars fixed on Toushi. 'Where is the RAT?' he said under his breath.

'Delayed?' Ben suggested, giving Caesar a pat beside him.

'Looks like a wild goose chase to me, Charlie,' Casper

whispered from where he lay. 'Zuba was never going to turn up.'

'Wait a minute,' said Baz. 'What's that sound?'

A buzzing noise grew increasingly loud. Looking around, they saw a single trail bike coming along the B3 from the west. Nearing the airstrip, the bike turned off the road and bumped across country until it reached the Cessna. It pulled up in front of Toushi Harada with a deliberate swerve of the rear wheel, raising a little cloud of yellow dust. Toushi looked at the battered Kawasaki and the young rider with an AK-47 strapped to his back. Toushi knew a bit about trail bikes – he'd ridden them in competitions as a boy and had even dreamed of becoming a world champion rider.

The Kawaski's rider looked at Toushi. 'You come to meet Colonel Zuba?'

'Yes,' said Toushi.

'You bring the money? The fifty thousand dollar?'

'Yes.' Toushi lifted the backpack.

'Show me.' The rider held out a hand.

'No.' Toushi pulled the backpack away from the rider's reach. 'Only for the eyes of Colonel Zuba. Where is he?'

'Get on,' the rider instructed, nodding to the pillion seat behind him.

Toushi hesitated.

'You want to see Colonel Zuba, you get on,' the rider informed him sourly.

With a sigh, Toushi strapped on the backpack, then climbed on behind the rider. They took off, first circling around the stationary Cessna, then making for the highway. Once on the hard black surface, the bike turned west and went zooming back the way it had come.

Duke Hazard watched the bike disappear from view. 'Something tells me Toushi's gonna be in a pile of trouble when Zuba discovers there's no cash in that backpack,' he said, stuffing a fresh sliver of gum in his mouth. 'And without us to back him up, Toushi's gonna be toast.' He began chewing furiously.

Charlie wished that they'd come equipped with a tracking device for Toushi. The drone was now their only way of keeping track of their colleague. He lifted the radio handset. 'Papa, Sinker has been picked up by a single trail bike. We've lost visual on him. Where's Bluey? We need a trace on Sinker. Over.'

'Bluey should be over your area in twenty. Over.'

'Twenty minutes!' Charlie exclaimed. 'Papa, the earth could have opened up and swallowed Sinker by that time! Over.'

'It's the best we could do, Oscar Zulu One. We were limited to a dawn deployment for Bluey. I'll let you know once we have images. Meanwhile, I'll get the Sallys in the air. They might manage a sighting. Over.' In case they were needed to airlift the GRRR men in

206

a hurry, both helicopters had spent the night on the ground, where they had set the team down ten kilometres to the north.

'Just keep those Sallys high enough not to be heard on the ground,' said Charlie. 'They could spook Bullseye if he hears them. Over.'

'Will do. In what direction was Sinker taken? Over.'

'Due west, along the B3. Over.'

'Copy that. I will advise. Sit tight. Papa out.'

'Roger that,' Charlie replied. 'Oscar Zulu One out.' He looked at Ben unhappily. 'I hope Toushi's good at dragging things out. We need time if we're to find him and Zuba.'

Ben nodded. 'Toushi's smart,' he assured Charlie. 'He'll figure something out.'

For ten minutes, the Kawasaki sped along the highway, only passing two other vehicles going the other way. Then the bike turned off onto a dirt road, which joined the highway from the south. Kawasaki and passengers bumped over the barren landscape for another ten minutes, passing a small village, after which the road petered out into a rough track. Before long, the bike came to a site of mud-walled ruins. Hidden by the early morning's long shadows, there sat the two Land Rovers and other RAT trail bikes. The bike slew to a halt, generating a cloud of dust. As Toushi climbed from the back, three armed men approached from the ruins.

Prior to joining GRRR, Toushi had been a backroom boy, a military computer whiz. He'd been loaned to the UN for that reason. But in Afghanistan, he had found himself with an assault rifle in his hand, on a secret and highly dangerous mission to rescue the UN secretary-general from the hands of Taliban insurgents. When he'd returned to Japan from that mission, his superiors had allowed him to opt out of future GRRR missions because they would likewise involve active service. But Toushi had thoroughly enjoyed that mission in Afghanistan. And to his surprise he had not been paralysed by fear when things had turned dangerous. He had remained calm, clear-headed and creative, even under fire. And so he had told his superiors he wished to continue in GRRR service.

Toushi knew he was again in danger – that his comrades had lost contact with him, and that for now he was on his own. But he was supremely confident that Charlie and the team would locate him if he stalled long enough. So, once again, Toushi found that he was calm, clear-headed and creative. As the armed men approached, he smiled at them.

The leader of the trio, a grey-haired man wearing a red beret and carrying a pump-action shotgun, smiled right back at him. 'So, this is the ivory trader?'

Toushi bowed to the man. 'I am, honourable sir, Toushi Harada, from Tokyo. You are Colonel Zuba?'

The grey-haired man laughed. 'No, I am not the colonel. Clearly, you do not know much about him.' His smile faded. 'I am Captain Chawinga, the colonel's deputy. Did you bring the money? Fifty thousand dollars?' He held out one hand.

'Colonel Zuba,' Toushi responded, folding his arms and keeping the backpack on. 'Colonel Zuba, if you please.'

Chawinga glanced at the backpack. 'Very well. You will follow me.'

'Oscar Zulu One, we think we've nailed them,' came Jinko's voice, which betrayed a mixture of relief and excitement. 'Over.'

'Oscar Zulu One receiving. What have you got for me, Papa?'

'Sally Two spotted two men on a bike on a back road at grid reference Romeo Eight. Over.'

All the GRRR men grabbed for their maps. Ben was the first to get his out, and together, he and Charlie found grid reference Romeo Eight.

'Looks about right,' said Charlie.

Ben nodded in agreement. 'About thirty clicks north-west of here.'

'Papa, that adds up to us. Over.'

'And to me,' Jinko replied. 'There are ruins of an abandoned Seventh-day Adventist Church mission not far from the sighting – an ideal hide-out for Bullseye. And hopefully for Game Boy and Oasis. I've ordered the Sallys to pull back to collect your team, and we'll have Bluey over the target shortly. Over.'

'Do we go in? Over.'

'Affirmative. On foot for the last click. The Sally One team from the south, Sally Two team from the north. Do you copy? Over.'

'Copy that, Papa. Over.'

'The Sallys are on their way. Papa out.'

'Oscar Zulu One out.' Charlie handed the handset back to Brian.

'Let's hope Toushi can keep the bad guys talking long enough,' said Duke Hazard, as he set about checking his ammunition.

Chawinga led Toushi to a set of steps that had been cut into the dry earth many years before by the builders of the mission. Chawinga pointed to the steps. Toushi nodded, then slowly made his way down the steps to a battered, partly open wooden door at the bottom. Chawinga followed close on his heels. Pushing the door open, Toushi stepped into a dingy underground space, the mission's former basement storeroom.

A little light slanted into the room from square ventilation holes dotted around the upper parts of the walls. A candle glowed yellow in one corner, and there sat Abraham Zuba on a bench. At home out of the daylight, Zuba had his transistor radio to his ear.

'Colonel, this is Mr Harada,' said Chawinga. 'The ivory trader.'

Toushi came to a halt several metres from the RAT commander, then bowed. 'Toushi Harada at your service, Colonel Zuba,' he said.

Zuba took the radio from his ear. Switching it off, he slipped it into a tunic pocket. 'So, Mr Harada, you are the Japanese gentleman who is prepared to pay me fifteen hundred dollars a kilo for ivory,' he said, looking up at Toushi.

Toushi produced a puzzled expression. He would attempt to stall Zuba by pretending not to understand him very well. 'Please? My English not good.'

'You will pay me fifteen hundred dollars a kilo. For ivory. Yes?'

Toushi smiled. 'Ah, fifteen hundred dollar. For ivory.'

'Good, good,' said Zuba, as his smile reappeared. 'But, tell me, why would you pay fifty per cent above the going rate? I would be happy to take your money, but I am curious to know why you would be so generous.'

'Please?' Toushi said, feigning helplessness.

A frustrated look now adorned Zuba's face. 'I will come back to that. Just show me the money.' He held out his right hand.

'No,' Toushi responded. 'Money after deal.'

Behind him, Chawinga reached for the backpack.

'No!' Toushi exclaimed, pulling away. 'Red dye in bag. Unless Toushi Harada unlock, dye go all over dollar.'

'What is he saying?' Zuba asked Chawinga.

'I think he said there is dye in the bag, Colonel, and unless he unlocks it himself, the dye will ruin the money.' Chawinga looked more closely at the backpack and the lock on the latch. 'It has a combination lock, Colonel,' he announced.

'Wrong combination, money all go red,' said Toushi, with the faintest of smiles. He was pleased with himself for thinking up this ploy on the spur of the moment. It had been purely by chance that the backpack had come equipped with the kind of small metal combination lock commonly used on luggage. But Toushi had an exceptional eye for detail and had noted the lock's presence, and had used it in his swiftly hatched plan to delay Zuba. Of course, there was no red dye device inside the backpack. But Zuba and his men didn't know that, and Toushi was banking on them not running the risk of trying to open the bag.

'Very tricky,' Zuba said with a chuckle. 'Very tricky

indeed, Mr Harada. You are a man after my own heart. A clever man should always take precautions.'

'We talk deal, then I give money,' said Toushi. 'Talkie talkie first. Money money second.'

'If that is what you want, Mr Harada,' said Zuba. 'Please, be my guest.' He pointed to the bench beside him. 'Sit. Let us talk.' He glanced up at his deputy. 'Chawinga, make Mr Harada some chai.'

In single file, the GRRR men tramped across the Tanzanian plain. The forty-degree heat rose up like a wall before them and made the blue hills in the distance dance and shimmer before their eyes. There was a faint breeze, but that breeze was furnace-hot on their faces. Their sunglasses helped to subdue the glare, but provided no protection against the force of the sun's rays that beat down on their helmets, shoulders and backs. Bathed in perspiration, their muscles aching with the effort of carrying their heavy loads, the men strode out as if they were merely going for a walk around the block. Years of ongoing fitness training and demanding operations in difficult conditions had prepared them for this.

Sally One had dropped Charlie's group south of the mission. Baz was out in front, leading the way, toting his Minimi as if it were as light as a feather. Charlie came next, with the Tanzanian Army's Sergeant Simma close behind. Simma had grown up in a village nearby and knew this area well. Ben and Caesar were next in line, with Caesar padding along contentedly on a long leash, tongue hanging out and panting to keep cool. Unlike humans, dogs don't sweat through their skin. They perspire through their feet via sweat glands around the hairless parts of their footpads. They pant to regulate their body temperature, moving cool air over the moist surfaces of their tongues and lungs.

Behind the labrador and his handler, Angus Bruce, Chris Banner and Casper Mortenson brought up the rear of the column. Big, tall Chris was carrying the GRRR team's second VHF radio on his back, along with his other equipment.

Charlie glanced at his watch. 'Ten minutes,' he said over his shoulder to Sergeant Simma. 'Pass the word – we should spot the mission in ten minutes.'

At this same moment, several kilometres north of the old church mission, Duke Hazard was in charge of the second half of the GRRR team as it made a southward forced march after being set down by Sally Two. Tim McHenry was out in front, with Hazard next and the Tanzanian Army's Lieutenant Roy coming not far behind to act as local guide and interpreter. Brian Cisco followed behind, with the aerial to the large radio in his back swaying back and forth with his every step. Willy Wolf was second last in this column, with Jean-Claude Lyon in the rearguard position.

To the south, as the members of Charlie's column tramped along at the cracking pace set by Baz, they could make out a stand of plane trees in the distance, which looked like a collection of ragged beach umbrellas. There were several large motionless shapes close by, partly obscured by the trees.

'Elephants,' Sergeant Simma called to the others as they walked, answering the question on all their minds. 'Those are elephants.'

'What are they doing?' Angus called. 'They seem to be just standing there.'

'They are in mourning,' Sergeant Simma replied.

'Mourning?' Angus responded.

'That is the location of the recent slaughter of elephants by Colonel Zuba and his men,' Sergeant Simma explained. 'The wildlife rangers brought in bulldozers and such things to bury the dead elephants in a mass grave. The families of the murdered elephants will come to the burial place often, to mourn the loss of their relatives.'

'They know that the dead elephants are under the ground there?' asked Chris Banner.

'Oh, yes, they know,' said Sergeant Simma. 'An elephant is a much more complex animal than most people think. Elephants will mourn the loss of family members for as long as six months. Unfortunately, poachers know this, and only have to come back to a killing ground such as this to find more elephants to kill.'

'Terrible shame,' said Angus. 'Poor wee elephants.' He cast his gaze to the distant group, whose members, young and old, remained stationary. It was as if they were carrying out a vigil over the place where their relatives had perished. 'Those majestic beasts do no one the slightest bit of harm, as long as we leave them alone.'

'Those particular elephants would not be in a very good mood if we went near them,' Sergeant Simma called to Baz, the column's leader. 'They know that it is humans who killed their kind. I think we should keep well away from them, or they could charge at us.'

'That'd be like being charged by an Abram tank,' Angus remarked. 'I've seen angry elephants trample people to death.'

'Stay downwind of them so that they do not acquire our scent,' suggested Sergeant Simma. He stopped to gauge the direction of the breeze, establishing that it was a northeasterly coming in from the Indian Ocean coast. 'We should keep to the west of them,' he said, resuming the march.

'Roger to that,' Charlie acknowledged. 'Baz, skirt around to the west of the pachyderms.'

'Of the what?' Baz returned.

'The pachyderms – the elephants.'

'Ah, gotcha,' said Baz, nodding. 'That's a roger.' The path that Baz now paved gave the grieving elephants a wide berth, and kept the party in a position that didn't allow their scent to reach the animals on the breeze.

Duke Hazard's group had come to a temporary halt. As Hazard checked his handheld GPS, the men around him drank from their canteens.

'We're on track,' Hazard announced, before taking a look at his watch. 'And on schedule. We'll be in place ahead of Zero Hour.'

'I hope our friend Toushi is keeping Zuba and his men talking,' said Jean-Claude Lyon.

'May I ask,' said Willy Wolf, 'how many armed men are we expecting to be with Zuba?'

'Zuba claims that he has an army of five hundred men,' said Hazard. He took a swig of water.

'The guy is all hat and no cattle,' said Tim McHenry.

This brought a laugh from Hazard and Cisco, who both knew what he meant. But the German and the Frenchman both looked mystified.

'What is the meaning of this "hat and no cattle"?' asked Willy.

'Friend,' said Tim, 'back where I come from – the great state of Texas – there are people who claim they're something they are not. These guys wear a mighty fine ten-gallon hat, just like a big-time cattle rancher. And they throw a pile of money around and tell you they got a million acres and a hundred thousand head of Short-horns back home. But when it comes down to it, those guys are lying through their teeth – they're all hat and no cattle. The same goes for Abraham Zuba. He don't impress me none. The guy is all talk.'

'That would seem to be true,' said Lieutenant Roy. 'From what the locals have been telling us, Zuba has perhaps thirty men with him. And a number of them are boys.'

'Boys with guns,' added Jean-Claude.

Duke Hazard was slipping a fresh piece of gum into his mouth. 'Sure enough,' he said, nodding. 'Even a boy with a gun can kill you.'

McHenry nodded. 'Ain't that the truth.'

'Okay, people, let's get this show on the road again,' said Hazard. 'We need to be in position to launch the assault on Zuba in fifteen minutes.'

'Oscar Zulu One and Oscar Zulu Two, from Papa. Bluey is in position. Over.'

'Oscar Zulu One copies. Over.'

'Oscar Zulu Two copies. Over.'

Charlie looked to the sky. The circling Heron UAV was much too high to be viewed from the ground. But its cameras could see all the way down into the ruins of the old Seventh-day Adventist Church mission.

'We have twenty-plus hostiles in the ruins,' Major Jinko advised. Sitting at his desk hundreds of kilometres away aboard *Canberra*, he was watching the live pictures from the Heron – close-up pictures of the mission. 'Could be more hostiles in cover. Over.'

'Papa, this is Oscar Zulu One,' said Charlie. 'Any sign of Sinker? Over.'

'Can't be sure if Sinker is there, Oscar Zulu One. Over.'

'Do they have pickets out? Over.'

'No pickets visible. There's little movement. Looking pretty sleepy down there. Both Oscar Zulus move in on my command. Over.'

'Roger that,' replied Sergeant Hazard. 'Over.'

'Roger to that,' echoed Charlie. 'Over.' He looked around at the men of his group. They were all lying in the undergrowth beside a snaking dirt track with their eyes focused on the ruins 300 metres away across almost clear ground. Ben was directly beside him, with Caesar stretched out full-length at his side, lapping up water from the aluminium cup that Ben held for him.

'Do you think we should send Caesar in first?' Charlie asked Ben. 'I doubt they've laid any IEDs, but he could serve as a diversion.'

Ben smiled approvingly. 'Good idea. Let's see how close we can get before I send him in.'

Charlie raised the radio handset to his mouth. 'Papa, from Oscar Zulu One. Permission to send in EDD in advance? Over.'

'That's a roger, Oscar Zulu One. Permission granted. He might draw some of the hostiles into the open. Inform me when he's in position and we can launch the assault. Over.'

'Roger to that. Out.'

'This is Papa. Do you copy, Oscar Zulu Two? Over.'

'Oscar Zulu Two copies,' Hazard advised. 'Out.'

'Papa out.'

Charlie pointed to the ruins. 'Ben, you and Caesar work your way around to the left, to that dead tree. Then send Caesar in.'

'Roger.' Ben stuffed Caesar's drinking cup into a pouch on his belt, then leaned close to Caesar and spoke softly to him. 'Okay, mate, time to play.'

Caesar's tail began to thump on the ground, and the look on his face seemed to say, *Let's go, boss! I'm ready for some fun.*

CHAPTER 19

Ben and Caesar crept across the dusty terrain on their bellies. This sort of belly crawl didn't come naturally to a labrador. They would do it briefly in play, but not over an extended distance. As part of his military training, Ben had taught Caesar the long-distance crawl. Once the pair reached the dead tree sitting beside the dirt track that led to the mission, Ben unclipped Caesar's leash and pointed to the ruins. 'Seek on, Caesar. Seek on!'

Caesar immediately rose up and trotted toward the mission. Behind him, Ben clicked on the personal radio attached to his bulletproof vest. 'EDD deployed,' he said in a low voice.

'Copy that.' Charlie's reply came through the earpiece in Ben's right ear.

Ben brought his compact Steyr assault rifle to his shoulder. It had a telescopic sight on top, through which he surveyed the ruins. If he spotted anyone in there taking aim at Caesar, he would not hesitate to take them out to protect his four-legged partner.

With his nose down, sniffing the ground for traces of explosives, Caesar continued to trot forward. When he came to a mud wall that had been eroded to half its original height by years of weathering, he stopped. On the wall in front of him, with one foot on the ground and an AK-47 in his lap, sat a boy soldier. A smile came across the boy's face. Calling back into the ruins, he came to his feet and approached Caesar.

Half-a-dozen more boy soldiers emerged from the ruins and hurried over, delighted and surprised by the sight of the labrador. Caesar eased his rear end to the ground, having picked up the scent of explosive chemicals on them. The boys gathered around and began to pat him. When one boy cautiously held out his hand, Caesar licked it. Giggling, the boy withdrew his hand, and the others laughed.

One of the older soldiers appeared at the mission's ruined gateway and, frowning, called to the others. As he spoke, one of the boys noticed the emblem of the rising sun on Caesar's fine metal collar and the words 'Australian Army'. The boy knew enough English to realise what this meant, and jumped back as if he had seen a ghost. 'This is a military dog!' he cried.

At that moment, the older soldier at the gate spotted movement a hundred metres beyond the group of boys. With fear suddenly etched on his face, he bellowed a frantic warning. Charlie, Angus, Chris and Casper, who had all crept closer to the mission, now rose up and ran toward the ruins. Seeing the RAT soldier bring his rifle to his shoulder, Ben pulled the trigger of his Steyr. The soldier let go of his rifle and dropped like a stone.

Baz, lying in cover, fired a warning burst from his Minimi into the air, over the heads of the boys with Caesar. Two of them threw themselves to the ground. The boy who had been the first to approach Caesar dropped his rifle and fearfully thrust his hands in the air. Two others threw away their weapons and ran – one went left, the other went right, heading for open country in panic. The remaining pair fled back into the ruins, still clutching their assault rifles.

Ben whistled to Caesar. It was one of his 'recall' whistles, this one meaning 'come back quickly'. Caesar immediately turned in a half-jump and bounded back toward Ben. By the time Caesar had returned to Ben at the dead tree, the four running GRRR men had reached the low wall. Casper was left in charge of the three boys who had remained in the open. On one knee, he kept his rifle trained on them as they lay with their hands behind their heads. From this position, he was also able to keep an eye on the soldier brought down by Ben, who was lying on his back, wounded, in the gateway.

Baz came loping up to join his comrades at the wall. Ben and Caesar were the last to do the same. As they did, bullets from several AK-47s flew overhead, fired at them from within the mission ruins. Charlie peeked around the corner of the broken wall, just in time to see a youth with an RPG launcher standing in the mission courtyard twenty metres away and aiming right at him. There was a *whoosh*! A tail of flame shot out from the launcher, and something small and dark emerged from its barrel.

'RPG!' Charlie yelled, ducking fast.

The rocket-propelled grenade flew over the men to detonate on the plain with a *whoomp*! In an instant, Charlie was up, carbine at his shoulder, ready to take out the soldier. But the soldier had dropped the RPG launcher and was running for cover, abandoning his weapon in the middle of the courtyard. Charlie held his fire. In the distance, from the rear of the mission, came the sound of more shooting. Duke Hazard's group had launched their attack from the north.

Hazard yanked a stun grenade from his belt, pulled the pin, then rolled the grenade around the corner and dropped to one knee, hugging the mud wall for cover. Seconds later, there was a flash of light, accompanied by a *whump*! Special Forces referred to stun grenades as 'flash-bangs', for they produced a blinding flash and a thunderclap of a *bang*. In an instant, Hazard was on his feet and rounding the corner, M-16 at the ready. He found a youth on his knees, head down, with his hands to his ears. The grenade's flash had dazzled the boy while the soundwaves had temporarily deafened him. The youth's AK-47 lay on the ground. Hazard kicked the weapon away, well out of reach.

'Take care of this guy,' Hazard instructed Brian Cisco, who had come up directly behind him.

'Sure thing.' The signaller grasped the disoriented youth by the collar, then dragged him back around the corner.

Ahead, Hazard could see steps leading down into the ground. Training his weapon on a closed wooden door at the bottom of the steps, he glanced back to see Lyon, McHenry and Wolf rounding the corner to join him. Hazard pointed to the stairs and waved for Jean-Claude to take the lead. Lyon brushed past him and descended warily. When he reached the bottom of the stairs, the Frenchman looked up at Hazard and the others. They were waiting at the top, keeping to one side to avoid any bullets which might come flying through the door.

'Go ahead, Lyon,' Hazard called in a hushed voice. 'Try the door.'

Carefully, Jean-Claude reached for the doorhandle. Turning it, he then pushed the door hard and flattened himself against the earth wall that lined the stairway. The door swung inwards. There was silence. No guns opened up from inside. And then a plaintive voice called from the darkness beyond the door. 'Don't shoot, boys. It is me, Toushi Harada.'

Hazard and McHenry trotted down the steps to join Lyon. Hazard patted the Frenchman on the shoulder. First Lyon, then Hazard and McHenry, dashed into the room with their weapons levelled. In the darkness, Lyon tripped over something on the floor.

'It is me!' wailed Toushi. 'It is Toushi Harada.'

Hazard whipped out his torch and shone it on the floor. Toushi was lying on his stomach with his arms taped behind his back. 'Are you okay?' asked Hazard, dropping to one knee beside his comrade.

'Yes, I am okay,' Toushi responded. 'Please untie me.'

Jean-Claude and McHenry shone their torches around the room. There was no one else there. One torch lit up an extinguished candle on the bench where Zuba had been sitting not long before. The other beam fell upon a backpack lying on the dirt floor with newspapers strewn around it.

'What happened?' asked Hazard. He swiftly put down his torch and shouldered his M-16, then reached for the knife on his belt.

'I keep up pretence of being ivory merchant as long as I could,' explained Toushi. 'But Zuba became suspicious when I could not say how I would ship ivory from this country. They opened my backpack –'

'And found nothing but newspapers,' said Hazard. He slit the tape binding Toushi's wrists.

'They had just finished tying me up when there was sound of gunfire. Zuba and another called Chawinga ran from room and left me here.'

'We must have missed them by seconds!' Hazard growled. 'Where the heck have they gone?'

Charlie and Angus vaulted the perimeter wall and ran across the courtyard toward the two Land Rovers parked beside the ruins. Behind them, Ben pointed to the wall and said to Caesar, 'Jump, mate! Jump!'

Caesar bounded over the wall, with Ben right behind him. For a moment, Caesar paused, waiting for Ben, and then, tail wagging, he ran at Ben's side. Back at the wall, Casper continued to watch over the young prisoners, and Baz and Chris kept their weapons trained on the compound.

The barrel of another RPG suddenly appeared around a corner and fired at the three running men and bounding dog. The rocket-propelled grenade flew by Charlie and Angus and hit one of the Land Rovers, which erupted in flames. Charlie, Angus and Ben all hit the ground, and Caesar dropped onto his stomach. The RPG launcher had disappeared from sight.

'Baz, RPG at your eleven o'clock!' Charlie yelled. 'He's probably reloading.'

'I'm on it!' Baz calmly sighted down his Minimi at the corner from where the RPG had fired.

Seconds passed before the barrel of the RPG reappeared around the corner. It was aimed in the direction of the men on the ground. But Baz was ready and waiting. A short burst from his Minimi hit the barrel of the RPG launcher, knocking it from its operator's hands. As soon as the launcher dropped, Charlie and Angus were on their feet and running. Around the corner they dashed. Finding the RPG operator on his knees, they took him captive.

Duke Hazard's voice came over all their personal radios. 'Sinker is secured. I say again, Sinker is secured, unharmed. But Bullseye is on the loose.'

From the distance came the buzzing sounds of trail bikes.

'They're getting away on bikes!' said Charlie. He pressed the 'talk' button on his personal radio. 'Chris, come to me. Now!'

When the big West Indian came loping up, Charlie told him to get Major Jinko on the radio. Banner made contact with Jinko, then handed Charlie the handset.

'Papa, from Oscar Zulu One,' said Charlie. 'Receiving? Over.'

'Loud and clear, Oscar Zulu One,' came the response from *Canberra*.

'Papa, we have secured Sinker, but Bullseye is on the run. Do you have a visual? Over.'

'Affirmative, Oscar Zulu One. Bluey is tracking five trail bikes with five riders and two passengers, heading north. Over.'

'Copy that, Papa. Over.'

'Suggest you use the hostiles' wheels to pursue once you've secured the compound. I'll keep you posted on the mobiles' position. Over.'

'Roger to that. Out.' Looking around the corner, Charlie saw that not only was the first Land Rover engulfed in fire, the flames had spread to the tyres and canopy of the second vehicle. Neither Land Rover would be of use to the team.

The two GRRR groups linked up and methodically searched the ruined mission for their targets. They took nineteen RAT prisoners, including the wounded man at the gate. He was treated by combat medic Willy, who advised Charlie that the man's wound was not life-threatening. But neither Zuba nor his deputy Chawinga were among the prisoners.

As their search of the ruins was being completed, Ben and Caesar came across a felt hat lying upside down in the dust. 'Akubra?' said Ben, stooping to pick it up.

Caesar, always curious, sniffed the hat in Ben's hand, then began to wag his tail furiously. Looking up at Ben, he whimpered, as if wanting to tell him something.

Ben knew what he meant. 'Come on, mate,' he said. 'Let's show Charlie what we found.'

Ben and Caesar quickly located Charlie inside the ruins, talking to Hazard and Lieutenant Roy.

Seeing them approach, Charlie sensed they were onto something. 'What've you found, Ben?'

'This.' Ben waved the hat in his hand, and Caesar jumped, trying to grab it between his teeth. 'Steady on, mate,' Ben responded with a smile, holding the hat out of Caesar's reach.

'What's got the dog so excited, Fulton?' asked Hazard.

'This hat,' Ben replied. 'It's an akubra. An Australian hat.'

'So, the dog's patriotic?'

Ben shook his head. 'Lucky was wearing a hat just like this the last time that Josh, Maddie and I saw him, on screen. Caesar has picked up Lucky's scent on this.'

'I'll be darned,' said Hazard. 'Is that possible? Could the dog remember Mertz's scent?'

'This is Caesar we're talking about, Hazard. Not just any dog.'

'I know, but . . .'

'Caesar remembers all our scents. He'd be able to recognise the scent of all the members of the GRRR team.'

'Does this mean that Lucky was here?' Charlie pondered aloud.

'Could be,' said Ben. 'Or one of Zuba's men recently souvenired Lucky's hat. The new owner's scent would also be here, but not strong enough to mask Lucky's. At least we know we're close to Lucky.'

'Okay, it's time we tracked Lucky down,' said Charlie. 'With luck, those trail bikes will lead us right to him.'

'A pity those Land Rovers are toast,' said Hazard. 'We could've used them.'

'Zuba's men left behind seven trail bikes. That's enough to carry us all if we travel light– except for Caesar.'

'You mean that Caesar can't ride a bike, not even as a pillion passenger?' joked Hazard.

'We need to commandeer ourselves a four-wheel drive,' said Charlie, ignoring Hazard's attempt at humour. He turned to Baz. 'Mate, you, Chris and Sergeant Simma take a couple of bikes back to the highway and find us a four-wheel drive, pronto.'

'A pleasure to oblige, oh mighty leader,' said Baz. He was in good spirits, for he knew that they were close to finding his good friend Lucky, at last.

231

Mr Omary Monson, his wife Mara and their four children were driving in their Toyota Landcruiser along the B3 on their way from Ushirombo to Mwanza when they came across three armed soldiers standing in the road. Mr Monson slowed the Toyota to a halt and worriedly watched as a sergeant of the Tanzanian Army came to his window.

'What is the problem here, Sergeant?' Mr Monson asked.

'I am afraid we need you to hand over your vehicle, sir,' said Sergeant Simma. 'As a temporary measure. The vehicle will be returned to you in due course, with the grateful thanks of your grateful government. Please now all get out. This is a matter of national security.'

'National security?' said Mr Monson. 'But what are my family and I supposed to do? You cannot leave us here in the middle of nowhere in the heat of the day.'

'We'll swap you, mate,' said Baz, coming to join Simma. He nodded to the three trail bikes by the side of the road, which he, Chris and Simma had used to get here.

'Bicycles?' said Mr Monson, appalled by the very idea.

'Trail bikes,' corrected Baz. He looked at the four boys on the back seat of the Landcruiser. Two of them appeared to be in their early teens. 'You and your boys can handle them, no problem. And your wife and the other two can hop on behind.'

'I think it a very good deal, father,' the eldest boy said enthusiastically. 'I have always wanted a bike such as those.'

'Be quiet, Zacharia!' Mr Monson growled. He looked at Baz and Simma. 'I do not wish to exchange my very expensive Toyota Landcruiser for three bicycles.'

Baz's eyes narrowed. 'Mate, it wasn't a request.'

'I am sorry, sir,' said Sergeant Simma apologetically, opening the driver's door.

But Baz wasn't apologetic – his mate was in mortal danger. He patted his machinegun. 'My friend Mr Minimi here says get out of the vehicle. Now!'

Lucky arched his back in a long stretch, then, with his bound hands in front of him, he began to walk. He'd badgered the guards until they had agreed to let him and his rangers out of the herdsman's hut for exercise. But because Zuba had only left four of his men to guard the prisoners when he took the remainder of his army south, those guards had only agreed to allow the prisoners out one at a time, to walk around the compound. In the late afternoon, Lucky was the last to be given a taste of exercise.

With just four guards to contend with now, Lucky was thinking seriously of attempting to jump them and free his men and himself. Two of the four soldiers were the regular guards, Sirum and Tonkei, men in their twenties or thirties. The other two were new recruits, including Legeny, the boy who had told Lucky he wanted to go home to his mother. These two youngsters would not pose a problem as far as Lucky was concerned. But the regular guards were a tougher prospect, and Lucky

The GRRR men moved slowly, carefully into position on the outskirts of the village of Kanda in low moon-light. All twelve members of the team were present. Toushi, dressed in his civilian wear, had been given his assault rifle and pack by his colleagues, and was ready to play his part in the rescue of Lucky Mertz. They had left Lieutenant Roy and Sergeant Simma back at the mission in charge of the prisoners. It was now up to GRRR to do what they did best.

To determine how they would go about this, the four sergeants in the group – Charlie, Ben, Hazard and McHenry – huddled together in the darkness. Charlie was in charge, but with the life of their friend Lucky in the balance, he wanted to be sure that the senior men in the team were in complete agreement about how they were to proceed.

'I say we go in hard with stun grenades and grab Lucky while they're all seeing stars,' Hazard said in a low voice.

'Only problem with that idea,' whispered Charlie, 'is that we don't know for sure that Lucky's in the village.'

'And if he is there,' said Ben, 'where in the village is he? We have to know precisely where he is before we go in with all guns blazing.'

'You got that right, Ben,' McHenry agreed. 'Somehow we gotta case the joint.'

'I suggest we send Caesar in with the camera,' said Ben.

'Can he operate okay in the darkness?' asked McHenry.

'Sure,' said Ben. 'Remember how good he was in Deep Cave in Afghanistan? Caesar doesn't need light to navigate. His nose is his radar.'

'Sounds good to me,' said Charlie. 'Kit him up, Ben, and let's get to it.'

It took several minutes for Ben to take the special equipment from his pack and prepare Caesar. First, he strapped a black Kevlar dog vest around his canine partner, before clipping a small video camera and transceiver on top of it. All the while, Caesar stood patiently as Ben placed the equipment on his back. Ben switched on a separate transceiver and booted up a laptop. Finally, he knelt beside Caesar and gave him a couple of dog biscuits to carry him over until he could organise him something more substantial to eat.

Once Caesar had devoured the biscuits, Ben spoke quietly to him. 'Caesar, we've got to find Lucky.'

Caesar's tail immediately began to wag. His expression seemed to say, *Our friend Lucky? Is that who you mean, boss?*

Ben smiled. 'That's right, mate – Lucky. Our mate Lucky.'

Charlie handed Ben the akubra, and Ben lay it upside down in front of Caesar. The labrador immediately put his nose inside the crown and began sniffing.

'That's it, mate, get a good whiff. I want you to find him for me. Find Lucky, Caesar.' Ben patted him vigorously, then pointed to the village. 'Seek on, Caesar. Seek on! Find Lucky!'

Without hesitation, Caesar leapt forward and went trotting into the night.

Ben joined the other members of the team in slipping night-vision goggles onto his helmet. From now on, the GRRR men would view their surroundings as if it were daytime, but in an eerie shade of green. Sitting cross-legged on the ground, Ben focused on the laptop's screen. Charlie, Hazard and McHenry clustered behind him to also watch the images on screen – images being sent back to the computer from the camera on Caesar's back.

Caesar quickly entered the village. With his nose to the ground, he skirted hut after hut. The voices of men, women and children came from within each, but Caesar ignored them all as he went in search of his friend Lucky. When he reached the palisade surrounding the cattle compound, Caesar's tail began to wag. He had picked up a familiar scent. Only a few hours earlier, Lucky had been doing his exercise walk on the other side of this palisade.

Caesar trotted along beside the curved wall of wood for ten metres, following the scent, until he saw a shadowy figure with a gun ahead. Dropping onto his stomach, Caesar sniffed the breeze. That breeze brought him the scent of a Tanzanian. Slowly, Caesar backed away a few metres and then rose up and trotted around the wall in the opposite direction. Although Ben could direct him via a small speaker in the transceiver on his back, Ben didn't dare speak in case his voice was heard by the RAT sentries. Caesar was making all his decisions unaided.

Again, an armed figure loomed in his path. And again Caesar halted, then backtracked. With the enemy preventing him from following the scent around the outside of the compound, Caesar decided to try to follow it on the inside. Urgently, he began to sniff the ground along the palisade. Choosing a spot where the ground was softest, he began to industriously paw the earth.

The GRRR men watched what was happening via the laptop screen, a hundred metres away. 'What's he doing?' Tim McHenry whispered to Ben.

'Digging,' Ben returned with an embarrassed grin. 'He's digging. The one bad habit I've tried to train him out of!'

'That bad habit might just pay off for us tonight,' said Charlie.

'You got that right,' said McHenry. 'Go, Caesar!'

Like a digging machine, Caesar spewed soft earth out

behind him. He dug until there was a hole deep enough for him to get his head beneath part of the wall. But the equipment on his back prevented him from crawling under. Undaunted, Caesar resumed digging. The next time he tried it, he was able to worm his way through.

Clambering out the other side, Caesar shook himself from head to paw to shed dirt. He looked around the emptied cattle compound and spied a herder's hut. Lowering his nose to the ground once more, Caesar soon picked up Lucky's scent. Following it, he trotted to the hut's entrance. For a moment he stood there looking at the locked door, then made a decision – he would follow the hut wall until he came to what he judged was soft ground. This he did and, again, he began to dig.

The hut walls weren't sunk as deep as the compound wall. Poles had been rammed into the ground, and the hut walls fastened to them. Caesar was digging at a gap between wall poles, and as a result, he only needed a hole fifteen centimetres deep to be able to gain entry to the hut. He wriggled through the hole, pulling himself to his feet inside the hut, and shaking off the dirt. Caesar saw the eyes of six men looking back at him and, without hesitation, went directly to one of the figures, jumping up at him and licking him on the face while his tail wagged furiously.

'I'm pleased to see you, too, Caesar my old mate,' Lucky said with a laugh. He pulled the labrador's head into a cuddle and patted him vigorously. 'Good old Caesar!'

'You know this dog, sir?' asked old Julius, amazed.

'Like I know my own brother,' Lucky replied. 'We've been in quite a few scrapes together, this dog and me.' He ruffled Caesar's neck. 'Haven't we, Caesar?'

In response, Caesar licked him on the mouth.

'Does this mean we are to be rescued?' Koinet asked from the other side of the hut, speaking for the first time since he had been returned to the captives.

'You just sit quietly and everything will be fine, Koinet,' Lucky responded.

Now, to the further astonishment of the rangers, Ben's voice emerged from the speaker on Caesar's back. 'G'day, mate.'

Grinning, Lucky looked into the infrared camera on Caesar's back. 'G'day yourself, Ben. Nice to know you're out there, mate.' As Lucky was aware from past experience, there was no microphone among Caesar's equipment, but he guessed that Ben could read his lips on his computer screen.

'You and your friends are to stay put and keep low, Lucky, and look after Caesar,' said Ben, before adding an instruction in a firm voice. 'Caesar, stay! Stay with Lucky!'

Looking like robots in their helmets and night-vision goggles, and moving slowly in a crouch, Charlie, Angus and Chris crept toward a village hut. These huts didn't have doors, just removable barriers of interwoven branches to keep out prowling predators. Inside each hut, a blanket covered the doorway. The oblong windows of the huts were at head height and had no glass in them, just a crisscross lacing of branches that permitted air circulation.

Standing beside one of these windows, Charlie poked a small infrared camera through a gap in the window lattice, recording what was inside. Pulling the camera back, he dropped to his good knee to review the footage. The occupants of the hut were all asleep. There were no weapons to be seen, nor any sign of the RAT. Charlie pointed to the next hut to do the same, and the quartet silently moved on.

At the same time, Hazard, McHenry and Cisco were checking huts on the other side of the village.

Like Charlie's team, they were looking for Zuba and his remaining men. Ben remained where the others had left him, watching his computer screen to make sure that Caesar and the hostages were okay. Meanwhile, a third GRRR team carefully approached the cattle compound. Baz was in charge of this team, and he was backed up by Claude, Casper, Toushi and Willy Wolf. Their task was to free and secure the hostages.

As the hostage rescue team snuck up to the cattle compound wall, Baz spotted the shadowy figure of a RAT guard standing ahead. Via hand signals, Baz instructed Jean-Claude to take care of the guard. Jean-Claude silently lay down his M-16, slid his commando knife from its sheath and crawled like a snake toward the guard. At the last moment, the guard – Tonkei – sensed that he was not alone. As he turned, raising his AK-47, Jean-Claude sprang like a lion. Within seconds, he was behind the much shorter guard, his knife to the man's throat.

'Not a sound, *mon ami*,' he whispered. With his left hand, Jean-Claude pulled the AK-47 from the terrified guard's hands and cast it aside. As Tonkei's mouth hung open, Jean-Claude removed the cigarette stuck to the guard's bottom lip. 'Cigarettes, they will kill you,' he whispered, before letting it drop to the ground.

As Jean-Claude hustled Tonkei to Baz and the others, a second guard suddenly appeared behind them.

'*Achtung!*' Wolf warned.

But this guard, only a boy, dropped his AK-47 upon spotting the heavily armed GRRR men, and ran off into the night in terror.

'Jean-Claude, keep an eye on your prisoner,' Baz instructed in a low voice. 'Willy, Toushi, Casper – with me.'

The four of them moved to the compound gate. A wooden bar was all that kept the gate closed. Carefully, Baz and Willy removed the bar and noiselessly lay it to one side. Pulling the gate back, the four men slipped into the compound. First Toushi, then Willy then Casper and finally Baz, sprinted to the front of the herdsman's hut.

'Anyone home in there?' Baz whispered through the door. 'I've got a special delivery for Mr Lucky Mertz.'

'Is that you, Baz?' came Lucky's voice.

'Too right it's me,' Baz returned, a grin spreading across his face. 'Who else would bother rescuing you, mate?'

'What took you so long?' said Lucky.

'Always complaining! You got much company in there?'

'Five of my rangers and a furry mutual friend.'

'No bad guys?'

'No bad guys.'

With the other three keeping low, their weapons at the ready as they surveyed their surroundings for signs of the RAT, Baz stood up and studied the padlock on the door. 'I'll have to blow the door, Lucky. You and your lot keep well back. And keep Caesar's head down.' Laying his Minimi against the wall, Lucky reached into one of his pouches for a small explosives charge made from C-4 plastic explosive that he'd prepared earlier.

'Have you secured the village yet?' asked Lucky.

'Not yet.'

'Well, then you can't blow the door yet. You'll alert Zuba's people in the village. Kerb your impatience, mate. You're too eager.'

'I know, I know,' Baz responded irritably.

At that moment, a dog began barking somewhere in the village. Baz froze and listened intently to the night as the dog continued to bark. Then, the sound of automatic weapons fire reached his ears.

'They're alerted now,' Baz said with a smile, before setting to work attaching the explosive charge to the padlock.

A small dog had appeared in Charlie's path and started barking at him. Chris Banner had lunged for the dog in an attempt to keep it quiet, but it had evaded him and run off through the village, yapping with every bound. The trio instantly prepared for a reaction from the huts, and sure enough, a man with an AK-47 appeared at a nearby hut window. Spotting them, he opened fire in their direction. As the gunman's bullets flew well wide of their mark, Charlie let off a three-round burst. Charlie never missed. The gunman had dropped from sight.

Charlie immediately reached for his belt and grabbed a stun grenade. Rising and dashing to the window from where the RAT had fired, he pulled the pin and dropped the flash-bang through a gap in the window lattice, ducking for the detonation. Seconds later, the barrier at the hut door beside Charlie was thrown aside and dazed figures came stumbling out into the night. One of those figures was carrying an AK-47. Charlie quickly stuck out one of his Zoomers and tripped up the man as he passed. As the African tumbled through the air, his weapon flew from his grasp.

The firing and explosion caused all hell to break loose in the village. Men, women and children emerged from their huts, running and shrieking into open country. The GRRR men kept low, and in a matter of minutes they snared six RATs among the panicking villagers. All surrendered without a fight.

'How many bad guys does that leave on the loose?' came Hazard's voice over their personal radios.

'Just two,' said Charlie. 'Zuba and his deputy. Search every hut.'

'You got it,' replied Hazard. 'They gotta be here someplace.'

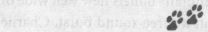

As Baz and three members of his detachment hunched beside the herdsman's hut, a dull thud came from the door as the C-4 exploded. As soon as the dust settled, Baz was on his feet and moving to the door. He'd done his job well – the explosive charge had neatly removed the padlock. Baz kicked open the door and found six men and a labrador sitting in the gloom, looking at him. Lucky Mertz was hugging Caesar, whose tail began to wag at the sight and smell of his friend Baz.

'Let's go, you blokes,' said Baz. 'We're getting you out of here.'

Led by old Julius, the Tanzanian rangers all came to their feet and moved to the door. Koinet came last of all.

Lucky, standing with Caesar at his side, waited for his men to leave, then held out his hand to Baz. 'This was the last place I expected to see you again, mate,' he said with a smile.

'Likewise, mate,' said Baz, shaking Lucky's hand. 'I hope we don't make a habit of this. I thought a good Special Forces operator like you could look after himself.'

'I can look after myself well enough, Baz, but I had to think of my rangers. If you hadn't come along tonight, I was planning to dig my way out.'

Baz laughed. 'Caesar dug his way in instead!'

Led by Charlie and Hazard, the teams made their way from hut to hut, checking for signs of Colonel Zuba and Captain Chawinga. Charlie's team had checked five huts and were approaching a sixth when Charlie saw a grey-haired man in a red beret disappear inside it. After the man failed to stop when Charlie called a challenge to him, the team burst in through the open door. They found the man sitting on the ground, singing to himself. The beam of Charlie's torch fell upon the man's shrivelled face. A shotgun lay beside him. Angus scooted past Charlie and grabbed the weapon, but the grey-haired man seemed unconcerned.

A message from Baz came over their personal radios. 'Charlie, we've got Lucky and his men. I've relocated them and Jean-Claude's prisoner to the outskirts of the village, at Ben's location.'

Charlie smiled with relief. 'Are they all okay?' he radioed back.

'Right as rain. Caesar's fine, too.'

'Keep them there, Baz. Ben, you and Caesar come to me. We've located Zuba's deputy. But there's no sign of Zuba. Caesar might be able to track him down.'

'On our way,' Ben responded.

By the time Ben and Caesar joined Charlie's team,

Charlie had lit the hut's kerosene lantern, filling the single room with a golden glow.

Charlie glared down at their latest prisoner. 'Where's Zuba?' he demanded.

Chawinga looked up at the GRRR men and smiled. 'You will never find him,' he said. 'This I do declare. He is too clever for you *mzungu*.'

'Where is he, old man?' Chris Banner demanded. 'Where is Zuba?'

Chawinga shrugged. 'You will never find him.' He chuckled to himself. 'Only the flies know where he is now.' He began to sing anew.

Angus looked down and saw a small transistor radio and a beret lying on the floor. 'A red beret, like the RAT wear!' he said, stooping to pick it up.

'Leave it!' said Ben.

Angus looked around at him in surprise. 'Why?'

'You'll mask the scent on it. If I'm not mistaken, that beret belonged to Zuba.' Ben led Caesar to the beret. 'Have a sniff of that, mate.'

Caesar dutifully sniffed the beret, then looked around at Ben with a quizzical expression on his face, as if to say, *Okay, now what, boss?*

'Follow the scent, Caesar,' Ben instructed. 'Find Zuba for us. Seek on, Caesar!'

Caesar immediately turned and led Ben from the hut. Leaving Angus to look after Chawinga, Charlie and Chris followed after them. With his nose to the ground, Caesar trotted through the village at a pace that required Ben and the others to jog to keep up. Before long, he led them to a dung heap outside the crowded goat compound. Made up of cowpats and goat droppings, this reeking pile was used by the villagers as a source of fertiliser for their few subsistence crops. A spade lay to one side. Here, Caesar stopped, as if uncertain. He looked up at Ben, as if to say, *The scent stops here, boss.*

Dropping to one knee, Ben said softly, 'See what you can find, mate.'

Nose to the ground, Caesar circled the dung heap, before returning to Ben. By this time, Hazard, McHenry and Cisco had joined the party. Again, Caesar stood looking at the dung heap, as if mystified.

'Don't tell me Caesar's lost the trail?' said Hazard, slipping a fresh piece of gum into his mouth.

'The trail led him to this dung heap,' said Ben, deep in thought. 'You know, in Afghanistan, the Taliban would use animal dung to try to disguise the scent of explosives. But they couldn't fool Caesar.' He gave Caesar a pat. 'Could they, mate?'

Caesar looked around at him briefly, before resuming his stare at the dung heap.

'So, what's Caesar telling you now?' Charlie asked.

'I think Zuba's under there.' Ben nodded to the dung

heap. 'See that spade? Zuba could have got someone to cover him with this stuff.'

Charlie snapped his fingers. 'Aha! His deputy said that only the flies knew where Zuba was. I reckon the deputy hid him under there.'

The others looked at each other with distaste.

'Okay,' Charlie said with a sigh. 'It'll take us a week to get the stink off us, but come on, you blokes, you know what we have to do.'

So, using the spade and their gloved hands, and grimacing at the foul smell, the men began to drag away pieces of dung. Before long, they uncovered a boot and a leg clad in camouflage trousers, followed by the rest of filthy, stinking Abraham Zuba.

'I always thought this bloke stank,' said Baz, pulling a face. 'But this is ridiculous.'

Ben bent down and patted Caesar with glee. 'You've done it again, Caesar! Well done, mate! Well done!'

Caesar's tail began to wag with delight, and he jumped up at Ben, seeking more praise.

'Yes, yes, you are a clever boy!' Ben said with a laugh, pulling Caesar's head into a cuddle.

Charlie was looking at the sad figure who now sat up, wiping dung from his face. 'Colonel Zuba, I presume?' Charlie reached down and removed the man's dark glasses. 'Commander of the Revolutionary Army of Tanzania and ivory poacher.'

'I demand a lawyer!' Zuba declared, turning his head away from the beam of Charlie's torch.

'You'll need one, buddy,' said Hazard. 'On a hostage-taking charge alone, you'll spend the rest of your life behind bars.'

Ben called over Brian Cisco and asked to be put through to Major Jinko. Taking the handset, he said, 'Papa, from Oscar Zulu One. Game Boy secured. Oasis secured. Bullseye secured. Request extraction by Sally. Over.'

'Roger that, Oscar Zulu One,' Jinko replied. 'Well done, Operation Pink Elephant team!'

Koinet pulled on and did up his new boots, smiling at Lucky and Chief Ranger Springer. 'They are a very good fit,' he said. 'Thank you.'

Lucky patted him on the back. 'Come on, Koinet, you can drive me to the airport.'

Springer watched Lucky and the young ranger tramp out the door of the Wildlife Service headquarters and climb into a four-wheel drive. As the vehicle drove off, Springer stroked his chin wistfully. He had taken Lucky's recommendation to accept Koinet back into ranger service.

'Koinet has learned a big lesson these past few weeks,' Lucky had told his boss. 'I think he'll make a fine ranger.'

There was a party at 3 Kokoda Crescent in Holsworthy. In a way, it was a combined welcome home and farewell party. Lucky had been home to New Zealand to see his parents and to reassure them he was fine, and had stopped over at Holsworthy on his way back to Tanzania to resume his job with the Wildlife Service. Joining Ben and his family, along with Lucky were Charlie and Baz. Nan Fulton had cooked a roast, followed by her classic pavlova dessert, and Ben, Charlie, Baz and Lucky had all cleaned their plates.

The grown-ups sat talking at the dining table after lunch. 'You mean to tell me that Captain Chawinga was Zuba's uncle?' said Nan.

'Turns out that way,' said Ben.

'Chawinga had ignored Zuba when he was a boy,' Lucky explained, 'but once Zuba was famous, and making money from ivory poaching, Chawinga joined his gang.'

'To exploit him,' said Baz.

Nan shook her head in disgust. 'I feel sorry for Zuba in a way. He was very badly treated as a child.'

'Feel sorry for all the elephants he butchered instead,' Lucky suggested.

'Too right!' said Baz.

'Of course,' Nan agreed.

'And feel sorry for the boys that Zuba and Chawinga kidnapped and forced to become soldiers,' added Lucky. 'At least those boys have been released and are on their way back to their families now.'

'Zuba took the easy way out, using violence, fear and intimidation to achieve his objectives,' said Charlie.

'And look what that got him. He and Chawinga are facing life in prison.'

'One more poacher removed from the picture,' Lucky said with a sigh. 'But there are plenty of others out there. We still need governments to outlaw ivory sales.'

'We should all petition the Chinese Government,' said Nan.

Everyone nodded soberly, before a young voice interrupted the conversation.

'Everyone come see!' Maddie called. 'Josh and me have stuff to show Lucky in the garden.'

So, the adults got up and trooped out into the garden. There, they found Josh and Kelvin Corbett.

'Dad, Kelvin and me want to show you something Sergeant Kasula taught us,' said Josh. 'We've been practising like mad.'

'Go ahead, Josh,' Ben said, not knowing what to expect.

As the adults watched, Kelvin bent down and, like a monkey climbing a tree, Josh clambered onto Kelvin's shoulders. Kelvin rose up gingerly. And there they were, with Josh standing on Kelvin's shoulders, both of them beaming as the adults applauded.

'It's all about balance,' said Josh.

'And teamwork, Mr Fulton,' said Kelvin. 'Isn't it cool?'

'It is cool, Kelvin,' said Ben, smiling wide.

'Teamwork's what us blokes are all about,' said Baz, nodding to his three best friends.

Josh jumped back down, and Lucky shook both boys by the hand. 'Well done, the pair of you,' he said.

'Sergeant Kasula decided we'd do better working together than fighting each other,' said Josh.

'And there's a lesson for life,' said Nan.

'My turn now,' called Maddie.

Everyone turned around to see Maddie leading Caesar out from behind the garden shed. She had tied one of Josh's long soccer socks under Caesar's head and filled it with other socks, so that it drooped from his chin.

Everybody laughed. 'Is that supposed to be a beard that you've given Caesar, Maddie?' Baz asked.

'Don't be dericulous, Uncle Baz!' admonished Maddie. 'It's a trunk. Caesar's an elephant. Look!' With that, she began to sway her head back and forth. 'Sway your head like I taught you, Caesar. Just like Maddie, sway your head.'

The ever-obliging Caesar swayed his head, making his trunk swing back and forth, bringing hoots of laughter from the audience.

'Who would ever think that elephant is the best war dog in the world?' said Baz, reaching for his phone to take a picture of the scene.

As he did, his, Ben's and Charlie's phones all rang at once. It was a text message from Liberty Lee in New York: *Rice for water*.

'GRRR needs us again,' said Ben.

'Calling in now,' said Charlie, immediately dialling Liberty's number.

Baz grinned. 'Sorry you can't join us on this one, Lucky!'

'I think you can handle it without me,' Lucky replied with a wink.

Caesar came at once to Ben's side, his makeshift trunk falling off. Looking up at Ben, he seemed to be saying, *Ready when you are, boss.*

LIST OF MILITARY TERMS

Abram M1 tank	main battle tank of US and Australian armies
AK-47	automatic Kalashnikov rifle, designed by Russian Mikhail Kalashnikov in 1947. Over 35 million have been produced.
ASR	air-sea rescue
bear	military intelligence personnel
Bell Jet Ranger	civilian helicopter sometimes used by police and military
Black Hawk, S-70A	military helicopter used as a gunship as well as a cargo and troop carrier
Blaser	sniper rifle; range 1500–2000 metres
brass, the	military slang for senior officers
Bushmaster	Australian-made troop-carrying vehicle, four-wheel drive; can carry eight troops plus a crew of two
C-4	plastic explosive frequently used by military
carbine	rifle with a shorter barrel than an assault rifle
clicks	kilometres

collateral damage	unintended injuries to neutral persons or damage to neutral property
copy that	'I have received' or 'I understand'
CPO	chief petty officer in the navy
doggles	protective goggles for war dogs
drone	unmanned military aircraft used for reconnaissance and bombing raids; officially known as an unmanned aerial vehicle, or UAV
DZ	drop zone
EDD	explosive detection dog
ETA	estimated time of arrival
ETD	estimated time of departure
extraction	pickup of troops from hostile territory by air, land or sea
fixed-wing aircraft	any aircraft that relies on wings for lift, as opposed to a helicopter
flat-top	aircraft carrier or helicopter carrier
French Foreign Legion	French Army unit used for special operations; traditionally accepts foreigners without asking questions

HALO	high altitude low opening; parachute jump from high altitude followed by freefall, with the parachute opening at low altitude
HE	high explosive
heelo	helicopter, also written as 'helo'
Hercules, C-130J	four-engine, propeller-driven military transport aircraft; pronounced 'Her-kew-leez' and often referred to as a 'Herc'
hostiles	enemy fighters
Hunter Corps	special forces unit of the Royal Danish Army
ID	identification
IED	improvised explosive device or homemade bomb
insertion	secret landing of troops behind enemy lines
insurgent	guerrilla fighter who does not use a regular military uniform or tactics and who blends in with the local population
intel	intelligence information
Interpol	international police organisation, with headquarters in France

Kalashnikov	see 'AK-47'
LHD	Landing Helicopter Dock ship of the Royal Australian Navy, such as HMAS *Canberra* and HMAS *Adelaide*; large helicopter carriers, with docking facilities for amphibious landing craft
loadmaster	crew member in charge of cargo and passengers in military cargo aircraft and helicopters
LZ	landing zone
M-16	American-made 5.56mm assault rifle
mess, the	a place in a military camp where troops gather to eat
Met	meteorological; weather
MRE	meal, ready-to-eat; a sealed military ration pack of pre-cooked food
operator	Australian SAS Regiment soldier
op(s)	military operation(s)
RAAF	Royal Australian Air Force
roger	'yes' or 'I acknowledge'
Romeo	latest version of MH-60 naval helicopter
round	bullet

Royal Marine Commandos	commando unit of the British Navy's Royal Marines
RP	rendezvous point or meeting place
RPG	rocket-propelled grenade
Seahawk	MH-60 Seahawk naval helicopter, the maritime version of the Black Hawk
Sea States 1–9	the international description of sea conditions, with Sea State 1 being 'calm', and Sea State 9 being 'phenomenal'
secure comms	communications that can't be intercepted
seek on	a handler's instruction to an EDD to find explosives
SOCOM	Special Operations Command
Special Air Service Regiment (SASR)	elite Special Forces unit in the Australian Army
Special Boat Service (SBS)	special operations unit of Britain's Royal Navy, specialising in small boat ops
Special Operations Engineer Regiment (SOER)	Australian Special Forces unit that specialises in military engineering and that trains and operates EDDs

special ops	special operations or secret missions
squadron	a small unit of Special Forces soldiers in the SAS; in the armies, air forces and navies of the world, the primary operational aircraft unit, often made up of a dozen aircraft or helicopters
Steyr	5.56mm assault rifle, Austrian design, made in Australia as the F88S Austeyr
Tiger	Eurocopter two-seat armed reconnaissance helicopter (ARH)
trooper	lowest rank in the SASR, the equivalent of a private in other army units
UAV	unmanned aerial vehicle, also known as a 'drone'
VC	Victoria Cross for Australia, the highest-ranking Australian military medal for gallantry
ward room	the officers' mess, or dining room, on a warship
XO	the Executive Officer, second-in-command aboard naval ships
yomp	forced march with full equipment
Zero Hour	the time set down by military for an operation to begin

FACT FILE

Notes from the Author

If you have read the first book in this series, *Caesar the War Dog*, you will know that a real war dog named Caesar served with Anzac troops during the First World War (1914–18). That Caesar, a New Zealand bulldog, searched for wounded men and carried water to them. Another war dog named Caesar, a black labrador–kelpie cross, served with Australian forces during the Vietnam War as an Australian Army tracker dog.

The fictional Caesar in this book is based on several real dogs of moden times – Sarbi, Endal and Cairo – and their exploits. Here are a few more facts about the real dogs, people, military units, places and equipment that appear in this book and inspired the stories in this series.

EXPLOSIVE DETECTION DOGS (EDDs)

The Australian Imperial Force used dogs during the First World War, primarily to carry messages. Sarbi was preceded by a long line of sniffer dogs used by the

Australian Army to detect land mines during the Korean War (1950–53) and, later, in the Vietnam War. In 1981, the current explosive detection dog program was introduced by the army's Royal Australian Engineer Corps, whose base is adjacent to Holsworthy Army Barracks in New South Wales. In 2005, Australian EDDs were sent to Afghanistan for the first time. A number have served there since and several have been killed or wounded in action.

SARBI

Sarbi, whose service number is EDD 436, is a black female labrador serving with the Australian Army. She began the EDD training program in June 2005 and graduated from the nineteen-week training course with Corporal D, joining the Australian Army's top-secret Incident Response Regiment (IRR) – now the Special Operations Engineer Regiment (SOER) – whose main job was to counter terrorist threats. In 2006, Sarbi and Corporal D were part of the security team at the Commonwealth Games in Melbourne. In April 2007, the pair was sent to Afghanistan for a seven-month deployment, returning to Afghanistan for their second tour of duty the following year.

On 2 September 2008, Sarbi and Corporal D were members of a Special Forces operation launched from a forward operating base a hundred kilometres northeast of Tarin Kowt. The operation went terribly wrong when five Humvees carrying Australian, American and Afghan troops were ambushed by a much larger Taliban force. In the ensuing battle, Corporal D was seriously wounded and became separated from Sarbi, who was also injured. Nine of the twelve Australians involved were wounded, as was their Afghan interpreter. Several American soldiers were also wounded in the battle. So began Sarbi's time lost in Taliban territory, a saga imagined in the first book of the Caesar the War Dog series.

After being 'missing in action' for thirteen months, Sarbi was wrangled back into friendly hands by a US Special Forces soldier. A month later, Sarbi and Corporal D were reunited at Tarin Kowt, in front of the Australian Prime Minister and the commanding US general in Afghanistan. Sarbi is the most decorated dog in the history of the Australian military, having been awarded all the medals that Caesar receives in *Caesar the War Dog*.

ENDAL

Endal was a sandy-coloured male labrador who was trained by the UK charity Canine Partners. He went on to qualify as a service dog and, in the late 1990s, was partnered with Allen Parton, a former Chief Petty Officer with Britain's Royal Navy. Confined to a wheelchair from injuries sustained during the Gulf War, initially Allen couldn't speak, so he taught Endal more than a hundred commands using hand signals.

In 2009, Endal suffered a stroke and had to be put

down. During his lifetime, Endal became famous in Britain, receiving much media coverage and many awards for his dedicated and loyal service to his master. A young labrador named EJ (Endal Junior) took Endal's place as Allen Parton's care dog.

CAIRO

Cairo is a long-nosed Belgian Malinois shepherd with the United States Navy SEALs (Sea, Air and Land teams), a unit within the US Special Operations Command. He was trained for insertion by helicopter, and by parachute, strapped to his handler, just like Caesar is in this book. In 2011, Cairo was part of SEAL Team 6, which landed by helicopter in a compound in Pakistan to deal with Osama bin Laden, the leader of the terrorist organisation Al Qaeda. Cairo's job was to go in first to locate explosives in the compound. Cairo and all members of his team returned safely from the successful mission.

SPECIAL AIR SERVICE REGIMENT (SASR)

The original Special Air Service was created by the British Army during the Second World War for special operations behind enemy lines, with the motto of 'Who Dares Wins'. In 1957, the Australian Army created its own Special Air Service Regiment, commonly referred to as the Australian SAS, two years after the New Zealand Army founded its Special Air Service.

Australia's SAS is considered by many to be the finest Special Forces unit in the world, and its members help train Special Forces of other countries, including those of the United States of America.

The top-secret regiment is based at Campbell Barracks at Swanbourne, in Perth, Western Australia. Because its men are often involved in covert anti-terrorist work, their names and faces cannot be revealed. The only exceptions to this rule are SAS members who receive the Victoria Cross. The unit is divided into three squadrons, with one squadron always on anti-terrorist duty and the others deployed on specific missions.

During the war in Afghanistan, Australian EDDs and their handlers have frequently worked with Australian SAS and commando units on special operations.

ZOOMERS

Charlie's high-tech Zoomers are based on real prosthetic 'blades' used by athletes.

TANZANIA AND THE FIGHT AGAINST IVORY POACHERS

Dar es Salaam and Mwanza are real cities in Tanzania. Other places described in this book, such as the town of Ushirombo and the nearby Kigosi Game Reserve, also exist.

The problems faced by the Tanzanian Government in trying to stop organised ivory poaching are very real and urgent. The figures relating to the loss of elephants quoted are real and official.

Chief Ranger Wallace Springer is inspired by a real person, an Australian.

THE UNITED NATIONS (UN)

The United Nations was founded in 1945 and its headquarters is situated in New York City, USA. To date it has 193 member states, including Australia, which fund its worldwide humanitarian and peacekeeping operations. The secretary-general, who is elected by its members, is the organisation's most senior officer.

Member states provide the UN's peacekeeping forces. UN humanitarian agencies include the United Nations Educational, Scientific and Cultural Organization (UNESCO), the World Health Organization (WHO), the World Food Programme (WFP), the International Court of Justice (ICJ or World Court), and the United Nations Children's Fund (UNICEF). Australia is currently a member of the UN Security Council, a body tasked with maintaining international peace and security.

About the Author

Stephen Dando-Collins is the award-winning author of more than thirty books, many of which have been translated into numerous languages. Most of Stephen's books are about military history and include subjects such as ancient Rome, the American West, colonial Australia and the First World War. *Pasteur's Gambit* was shortlisted for the science prize in the Victorian Premier's Literary Awards and won the Queensland Premier's Science Award. *Crack Hardy*, his most personal history, received wide acclaim. He has also written several titles for children and teenagers, including *Chance in a Million*, the Caesar the War Dog series and *Tank Boys*. Stephen and his wife, Louise, live and write in a former nunnery in Tasmania's Tamar Valley.

For more on other books by Stephen Dando-Collins, including books about Australian, American, British and ancient Roman and Greek military history, go to www.stephendandocollins.com.

WATCH OUT FOR BOOK 4

IN THE

CAESAR THE WAR DOG

SERIES

COMING SOON

STEPHEN DANDO-COLLINS

CAESAR
the war dog

AVAILABLE NOW

STEPHEN DANDO-COLLINS

CAESAR
the war dog

operation
blue dragon

AVAILABLE NOW

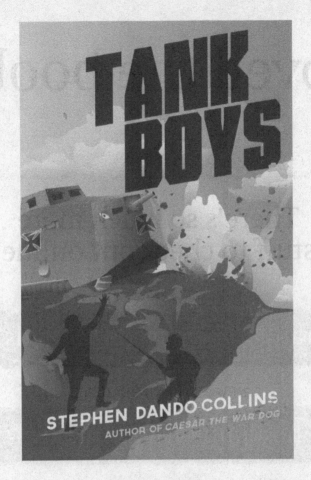

AVAILABLE NOW

Loved the book?

There's so much more stuff to check out online

AUSTRALIAN READERS:

randomhouse.com.au/kids

NEW ZEALAND READERS:

randomhouse.co.nz/kids

wouldn't put it past either of them to spray the hut with bullets and cut down his rangers if he tried anything out here in the open.

If he were to keep his men safe, Lucky knew that he would have to plan carefully. While he walked, either Sirum or Tonkei would walk behind him, cradling his Kalashnikov. The other would stand outside the compound with his gun poking through a gap in the wall of branches and trained on Lucky.

As Lucky walked around and around the oval compound, he studied it. The walls weren't too high to be climbed. The soil underfoot was sandy and loose. One of the plans he was considering involved digging his way out of the hut. But he reckoned he could only do that successfully under the cover of night, when most of the guards were asleep and no one could see what he was doing. He decided that his best bet was to wait for nightfall before he set an escape plan in motion.

But as Lucky walked, his heart sank. The sound of trail bikes reached his ears. Gradually, the buzzing grew louder, and Lucky cursed to himself. It sounded as if Zuba and the rest of his men were returning. Tonkei, the guard with him, heard the sound, too, and ordered Lucky back to the hut. Lucky had just reached the hut door when the compound's wooden gate opened, and in walked Koinet and Captain Chawinga. Koinet was barefoot and unarmed, and Chawinga, his shotgun in one hand, was pushing Koinet along in front of him.

'Throw this rotten fish back in with the others,' Chawinga instructed Tonkei. 'He is no soldier. When the bullets were flying, he was crying like a baby.'

Lucky looked at Koinet. The embarrassed youth dropped his eyes to the ground. And then the pair of them were shoved into the herdsman's hut and the door was locked behind them. Koinet was once more one of the prisoners.

'Oscar Zulu One, from Papa. I have seven hostiles joining with several more hostiles at grid reference Tango Four. Over.'

'Copy that, Papa. Tango Four,' Charlie replied from the front seat of Mr Monson's Landcruiser. Beside him, Baz was at the wheel. Ben, Caesar and other members of the GRRR team were packed into the back of the vehicle. The rest of the team, including Toushi, followed behind on the four trail bikes. 'Are the hostiles still mobile? Over.'

'Negative. They've halted at a small village. With luck, they're planning to stay put for the night. Over.'

'Copy that. We'll approach on foot. Over.'

'Roger that. Papa out.'